*"Oh, Cole, [...]  crying. I t[...] wrong."*

Without hesitat[...] took the baby from Rachel. He placed the screaming infant against his bare chest. With a voice that was soft and low, he stroked her back up and down as he swayed back and forth. After a few moments there was a contented sigh that brought a smile to Cole's mouth.

Rachel was amazed. "Why wouldn't she do that for me?"

"I think eventually she would have."

Cole gently laid the sleeping baby in her crib and stood back as Rachel tucked a light blanket over her. He should just leave, but he couldn't seem to stop watching Rachel with the baby. As much as he'd tried to stay detached from Hannah, when he'd held her it had been as if she'd reached her tiny hand into his chest and grabbed hold of his heart. He worked to draw air into his lungs and he looked at Rachel.

She

Dear Reader,

Long before I became a published author I was an avid reader of romance. Couldn't get enough books, and the traditional romance was such a mainstay in my life—in a lot of our lives. These books take us to a place away from our daily routines and problems and help us escape into a fantasy world…for a little while, anyway. And as a writer, I am able to create that wonderful make-believe world.

My story takes place in Ft. Stockton, Texas, where a single woman, Rachel Hewitt, tries to keep her family ranch going with the help of an unusual cast of characters: the over-the-hill ranch foreman, Cy, an abandoned teenage boy, Josh, a darling infant girl, Hannah and a drifter, Cole Parrish. Cole tries to move on, but something always comes up to stop him from leaving the Bar H Ranch.

For too many years, Cole has tried to outrun the sadness from his past, but when a newborn is literally dropped on the doorstep, he can't run away this time.

Enjoy,

*Patricia Thayer*

# PATRICIA THAYER
*The Rancher's Doorstep Baby*

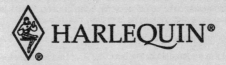

TORONTO • NEW YORK • LONDON
AMSTERDAM • PARIS • SYDNEY • HAMBURG
STOCKHOLM • ATHENS • TOKYO • MILAN • MADRID
PRAGUE • WARSAW • BUDAPEST • AUCKLAND

ISBN-13: 978-0-373-17488-1
ISBN-10:     0-373-17488-8

THE RANCHER'S DOORSTEP BABY

First North American Publication 2008.

**Patricia Thayer** has been writing for over twenty years, and has published thirty books with Silhouette® and Harlequin®. She has been nominated for various awards, including a National Readers' Choice Award, a Book Buyers Best and a prestigious RITA® Award. In 1997 *Nothing Short of a Miracle* won the *Romantic Times BOOKreviews* Reviewers' Choice Award for Best Special Edition.

Thanks to the understanding men in her life—her husband of over thirty-five years, Steve, and her three grown sons and three grandsons—Pat has been able to fulfill her dream of writing. Besides writing romance, she loves to travel—especially in the West, where she researches her books firsthand. You might find her on a ranch in Texas or on a train to an old mining town in Colorado, or even on an adventure in Scotland. Just so long as she can share it all with her favorite hero, Steve. She loves to hear from readers. You can write to her at P.O. Box 6251, Anaheim, CA 92816-0251, or check her Web site at www.patriciathayer.com for upcoming books.

### In the cowboy's arms...

Imagine a world where men are strong and true to their word…and where romance always wins the day! These rugged ranchers may seem tough on the exterior, but they are about to meet their match when they meet strong, loving women to care for them!

If you love gorgeous cowboys and Western settings, this miniseries is for you!

Look out for Patricia's next
WESTERN WEDDINGS book,

*A Bride for Wandering Creek Ranch*

available in April only from Harlequin Romance®.

# CHAPTER ONE

IT WAS time to move on.

Cole Parrish spread the fresh straw around the horse stall. In truth, it was past time to make his departure. He'd never stayed anyplace this long. Four months he'd been at the Bar H Ranch. After the heart attack of the foreman, Cy Parks, Cole couldn't leave the owner to fend for herself all alone.

He braced the pitchfork against the railing and pushed his hat back. The familiar restlessness gnawed at his gut, urging him to leave. He was getting far too attached to this place but the sooner he got out of here the better. The last thing he needed was more memories to carry away with him. He had enough of those to last a lifetime.

That was why he had to go now. And he had to tell Rachel Hewitt. Today.

Determined not to put off the task any longer, Cole walked out of the stall and through the barn. Outside, he looked toward the two-story frame ranch house across the compound. At one time it had been painted white, but like the rest of the place, the structure could use a new coat of paint along with a few repairs.

It would only take him a couple weeks to do the job... He shook his head. No. This wasn't his problem. He was leaving.

Before he reached the house, a young Rachel Hewitt came out on the porch. As on every other day she wore her usual work clothes—faded jeans and a man's shirt. Her long, raven mane was tied back in a long braid, exposing her pretty oval face. She was tall and solidly built, but there was something about her expression that suggested a fragile quality. His gaze met her golden-brown eyes and he felt his chest constrict, making it difficult to draw a breath.

He definitely had to leave. Soon.

"Rachel," he called as he approached her. "If you have a minute, I need to talk with you."

"What is it, Cole?" She gripped the porch post and smiled, but it didn't hide her fatigue. He doubted she'd gotten much sleep, what with running the house and doing the work of a ranch hand. Not that anything had changed since her father's death two years ago. He'd heard stories that old Gib Hewitt had run the Bar H from his wheelchair, but Rachel had been the one who did the physical work.

Cole had stayed so long because he knew Gib had given power of attorney to a lawyer until his daughter turned thirty. Rachel couldn't afford to pay much to ranch hands and Cole couldn't allow her to struggle on alone. That was the reason why his leaving would be so hard on her. But he had to do it.

He didn't do permanence…not anymore.

He stood at the bottom of the porch steps. "I'm giving my notice. I'll be leaving in a week," he said straight out.

He watched as her eyes widened in panic, then she quickly masked it. "You said you'd stay on a while. You know Cy can't do the work by himself."

Cole caught himself fighting a smile. "You better not let him hear you saying that." Cy Parks had been at the Bar H for nearly thirty years. She was right. He wasn't capable of handling it all by himself anymore. But this ranch wasn't big by Texas standards, a three-man operation at best. "Since spring roundup is over, things should be quiet for a time. He can manage feeding the stock. That should give you time to hire someone else."

Rachel didn't want to hire someone else. For one thing, she couldn't afford to. She wasn't even sure how much longer she'd be able to pay Cole. Although he was a drifter, she trusted the man. He was a hard worker. He was the one who'd been with Cy when he had his heart attack, giving him CPR and saving his life. Cole had kept him alive until the ambulance had arrived from town.

"There's no one else to hire. Most of the available men have moved onto the bigger operations around San Angelo."

"I'm headed there, too."

"Look if it's the money…"

He shook his head. "Just need a change of scenery. I'll work to the end of the week and if you like, try to find a replacement."

Cole Parrish was a handsome man, with his dark hair and piercing gray eyes. There were times when she saw such sadness in their depths, it made her want to cry. He must have his reasons for leaving, and she shouldn't try to stop him. "Thank you, Cole. That would be a big help."

He tipped his hat, then turned and walked back toward the barn. Rachel couldn't help but watch his departure with appreciation. A chambray shirt covered his wide shoulders but it couldn't hide his rock solid build. Years of rough ranch work showed in the muscle definition across his back and slim waist. He had a loose-hipped gait that showed off some attitude. All cowboys had a little cockiness about them. A gush of heat washed over her, making her insides ache. Since the day Cole Parrish had arrived at the ranch, she'd experienced this feeling many times.

Definitely Gib Hewitt would not approve. Rachel caught her breath and turned away. She'd loved her father, but he'd ruled with a strict hand when it came to his daughters. He'd lectured often to her and her younger sister, Sarah, on the evils of the world. Although he'd never said it to her face, she knew he'd been afraid they'd end up loose women like their mother.

Georgia Hewitt had left them when Rachel was ten and Sarah only five. Rachel tried not to hate her mother, but the abandonment she and her sister had felt never left them. After high school, Sarah was eager to leave and had begged Rachel to go away with her. In the end, Rachel couldn't desert her father and Sarah ran off to follow her dream.

Now, Sarah and her father were both gone. Rachel blinked away the threatening tears and walked into the house. Soon she'd be running the ranch on her own. That frightened her.

It also excited her.

At supper time Cole forced himself to walk through the back door just as he had for the past months. It was so familiar—too familiar. After this week, no more. No more seeing Rachel's smile and the special touches she added to everything.

Besides cooking the meals and caring for the house, she'd climb on a horse and move cattle just like any of the men. She put in twelve-hour days and never asked anyone to do a job she wasn't willing do.

Cole hung his hat on the rack, and stepped inside the dreary kitchen. Like the outside of the house, the walls needed paint. The linoleum was worn through to the pattern and the cabinet doors needed repair. Despite all that, the room was spotlessly clean.

At the stove, Rachel turned toward him and smiled. It sent a jolt of awareness through him. He found he'd been looking forward to seeing her. A man could get used to meeting this woman at the end of the day.

Just not him.

"Rachel." He nodded as he made his way to the table set for three.

After they sat down Rachel spoke. "Cole, I want

to thank you for helping me out these past months. It was wrong of me earlier to try to get you to stay on. You have been more than generous with your time."

Why did she have to be so nice? "You're welcome. If there's anything I can help you with before I leave, let me know."

His gaze met hers and a new stirring erupted in his gut. Desire. He could see it mirrored in her eyes, too. He glanced at her breasts, watching the rapid movement of her breathing. His common sense told him to stop, but his hunger wouldn't let him. At that moment a noise pulled his attention away as Cy came through the back door.

The old guy ambled to the table. His thin white hair was combed straight back, his face tanned and weathered by years of being in the sun, and his broad smile, causing tiny lines to form around his hazel eyes. On his doctor's orders, he'd lost weight in the past month and changed his diet.

He hitched up his too-big jeans. "Well, it looks like I didn't miss anything."

"As if you'd be late for a meal," Cole murmured, then walked to the refrigerator and took out a pitcher of water. He filled the glasses as Rachel set roasted chicken, mashed potatoes and garden-fresh green beans on the table.

"Darlin', I've died and gone to heaven," Cy said.

"Oh, Uncle Cy, you say that no matter what I cook," Rachel said as he held out her chair.

"I won't lie and say I don't miss your fried chicken and gravy."

Rachel smiled. "I'll try to come up with a way of fixing it so it will be healthy for you."

Once everyone was seated, the foreman said the blessing. "Lord, thank you for the food on this table. And for Rachel who takes such good care of us. Amen." He raised his head and reached for the potatoes. "Now, let's eat."

After serving himself, he passed the bowl to Rachel. "Thank you, Cy, for the kind words. But we all work hard around here."

"We get paid," Cy said, pouring gravy around his plate. "You do so many extra things for everyone. You don't have to wash my clothes or repair the rips and tears, but you do."

"You've just lost so much weight. Besides, I like to sew," she protested.

"I know," Cy said. "You make the prettiest quilts in the county. You ought to take 'em to one of the fancy shops in San Angelo." He glanced at Cole. "I've been tellin' her she'd make a lot of money."

She shook her head. "I donate them to the church."

The older man frowned. "And they turn around and sell 'em and make all the money. Money you need for yourself."

Rachel stole a glance at Cole. He didn't seem interested in the conversation. But that didn't stop Cy.

"You know I worked for your daddy for a lot of years, and he didn't always treat you fair and square."

Rachel felt heat rush to her face. "Father wasn't in good health and…"

Cy shook his head. "Stop making excuses for

him. He made you and your sister pay for your mother leaving…"

"Cy…please," she pleaded.

"She was your mama, Rachel, and your father drove her away, just as he did Sarah. You got this place to hold together…and you can't do a dang thing unless you get permission from that city lawyer." He took a bite of his food. "Thank goodness that's nearly at an end."

Rachel placed her fork on her plate. She didn't want to argue with Cy. What good would it do? Her mother, father and sister were all gone. She couldn't change any of that. "I don't want to talk—" She stopped, then pushed back her chair and got up. "If you'll excuse me," she said, then turned and walked out of the kitchen.

Cole fought to keep from going after her. But what could he say to her? He'd known men like Hewitt. He'd grown up with a disapproving parent, too. Nothing he'd done could please the man, so he'd finally stopped trying.

Cy looked across the table at Cole. "Now, don't you go lookin' at me like that."

Cole played dumb. "What way is that?"

"Like I just pulled the wings off a butterfly. That girl needs to rid herself of years of guilt her father hammered into her." The old man pointed to the doorway. "Have you looked at Rachel? She's afraid to be a woman 'cause her daddy made her feel ashamed of the fact she is one. I've stood back for too long and watched it. But that bastard has been gone for nearly two years and Rachel is still afraid to live. She's a beautiful woman. Someone needs to make her realize that."

Cole didn't want to hear any more. "I think Rachel needs to worry about surviving, and she'll do just fine." He took the last bite of food, then carried his plate to the sink.

"You're just saying that so you won't feel guilty when you leave here."

The old man's words hit home, but he still had to go. "I was hired for the roundup and I've stayed on a few extra months."

"And I appreciate you taking on my load."

"It wasn't a problem, but now, I've got a job waiting for me in San Angelo."

Cy didn't argue the point. He just finished his meal, then carried his plate to the sink. He leaned against the counter and studied Cole. There was no doubt the foreman had something else to say.

Cole stared the other man down. "All right, are you going to try to get me to stay?"

"No, you have to decide that for yourself." The old man gnawed on his lower lip as if choosing his words carefully. "I'm just wondering what you're running from."

Rachel had learned a long time ago that tears didn't help anything. They hadn't stopped people she loved from leaving her. Now, she was alone. She had no husband, no family to help her through this rough time. All she had was the ranch, and her own determination to keep it.

She changed into her nightgown and robe, then went into the bathroom and washed her face. She still needed to clean up the supper dishes.

Rachel went downstairs and walked through the large living room. The hardwood floors gleamed with polish, but an old rug in front of the barren fireplace was worn, as was the furniture. This was her home. She just had to think of a way to hold on to it, despite the lawyer's dismal picture of her financial future.

She walked through the dining room, then into the kitchen. She stopped when she saw Cole standing at the sink, his sleeves rolled up and his hands buried in dishwater.

A blush quickly spread over her cheeks. She didn't want to deal with anyone tonight, especially Cole. For a second she wanted to turn around and flee, but she lost that chance when he glanced over his shoulder and saw her.

For a moment they just stared at each other. His gray eyes locked with hers and she couldn't seem to take a breath.

He cocked his head, causing his inky-black hair to fall across his forehead. "Well, don't just stand there, grab a towel."

She managed to snap out of her trance. "You shouldn't be doing those." She went to his side, surprised when he didn't step aside.

"It's not a problem," he said as he rinsed the flatware, and placed them in the dish drainer. "I discovered it's a good way to clean the dirt from under your fingernails. You can dry."

"But this isn't your job."

He stopped and glared at her. "Why not? Haven't I seen you climb on a horse and help round up cows? Let's not split hairs here, Rachel. Besides, my hands are already wet."

Reluctantly she picked up the towel on the counter.

Cole had hoped to be finished before she came back downstairs. He hadn't wanted to end up in this situation with the house quiet and Rachel Hewitt dressed in a nightgown and robe, her long silky hair flowing down her back. He felt the heat move over his skin just because she was near. She made him remember what he tried so hard to forget. What he'd lost so long ago.

"I'm sorry about earlier," Rachel began, her voice husky. "Cy means well…"

Cole put a plate into the water, recalling how he'd almost gone upstairs and checked on her, but realized he'd be playing with fire.

Eighteen months ago, he'd made a couple of rules for himself. Not to get involved, especially with a woman like Rachel, and not to hang around any one place for long. He'd already broken one rule, and had no intention of breaking another.

He shrugged. "It's none of my business." The less he knew about her, the easier it would be to walk away.

"You still had to be uncomfortable. For that, I'm sorry."

"You and Cy are like family. I know he cares about you. He's just worried about you running this ranch by yourself. It's a big job."

She raised her pretty chin. "I've managed so far."

He rinsed another glass. "Is there any other family member that might be willing to help out?"

She shook her head as she stacked a plate on the counter. "My father didn't have any family."

Cole knew what it felt like to love someone and have them walk out of your life…for good. The tightness in his chest told him he was getting too close to memories, and the past that he desperately fought to keep buried. He pushed away the threatening emotions.

"Then we'll have to find someone you can trust to help run this place."

"I can't pay that much," she offered. "My father didn't save a lot. There's not enough to pay a decent salary. At least we did well with the sale of the spring calves, so the mortgage is paid ahead."

Cole knew that a lawyer, Lloyd Montgomery, controlled the money. But dammit, you couldn't run a ranch from a desk in town. Not even when you owned the neighboring property.

Don't get involved in this, Cole told himself. You're leaving at the end of the week. "There are other ways to make the ranch pay off." Finished with the dishes, he wiped his hands on the towel. "There are thousands of dollars to be made by allowing hunters on your property. You should think about it."

She nodded. "Father never shared much of the ranch business with me, and as you already know, I don't have control…yet. That will change soon. So lately, I've been going over things, trying to learn my way. Lloyd Montgomery thinks I should sell it all."

Cole frowned. "Why is that?"

"He doesn't think I can deal with everything myself."

Cole snickered. "What does he think you've been doing the last few years, having a picnic?"

That brought a smile to her face and his breath caught in his chest. She was strikingly beautiful and she had no idea.

"I'll need to do something to supplement my income, or I could lose it all." She was silent for a few seconds, then she said, "I was going over things in my father's office and found a letter from a windmill company that asked about leasing some land." Her large eyes locked with his. "When you have some time, would you look at the letter?"

"I guess it wouldn't hurt." He glanced at his watch. "How about now?"

Rachel set down her towel and together they walked through the house into a small office off the living room. A large desk took up most of the area, and like the rest of the place it was clean and orderly.

Rachel went to the file cabinet and took out a manila folder. She removed a letter and handed it to Cole.

He glanced at the letterhead. It was from 21$^{st}$ Century Windmill Company, located in San Angelo, Texas. The letter stated that the company had already done a survey of the Bar H's land and found that the rocky ridge mesa was ideal for windmills. Cole knew the area. It wasn't much good for anything else, not even cattle. The company had requested an agreement to use the land.

"Has your lawyer made any contact with them?" He glanced through the folder and found nothing else.

She shook her head. "No. I found this in the wastepaper basket. I don't think Monty thought the idea was a good one. What do you think?"

He didn't want to sway her, but he didn't understand why good old Monty had ignored what seemed to be a decent money-making idea. "It wouldn't hurt to listen to what they have to say. In a few weeks you'll take over the ranch, so why not just wait until then?"

"So, this is legitimate?" she asked.

He nodded. "It sounds similar to an oil lease. That's where the landowner is given money up-front from the company—in this case it's a windmill company. They come in, construct windmills and give the owners a percentage of the profits." He smiled. "Rachel. You could not only get money for the leased land, but for the electricity they produce and sell to the surrounding areas."

"So it's a good thing?"

"It could be very good. But you need to contact this 21$^{st}$ Century and let them know you're interested. No matter what the lawyer says, you're more than capable of dealing with these people…" He glanced down at the name. "This Douglas Wills." He handed the letter to her. He inhaled her fresh scent. No perfume could ever be as intoxicating.

Rachel raised her head and looked up at him. Her face was void of makeup, allowing him to see the tiny freckles scattered across her nose. Her eyes were amber, fringed with long dark lashes. His body warmed as desire spread through him. He tried to ignore it, but she was too close, her mouth too inviting. He found he wanted a taste. He heard the quickening of her breathing.

Then she spoke his name. "Cole…"

Blocking out logical reasoning, he lowered his head to hers, anticipating the kiss. Just to taste her, he promised. Just once he wanted to get lost in her innocence…her sweetness.

He was quickly brought back to reality by the sound of a car. Rachel jumped back. He should have been relieved but what he felt was frustration.

As Rachel went to the window Cole followed, amazed at how close he'd come to making such a huge mistake. He couldn't mess around with someone like Rachel and walk away. That would be too cruel.

The sun was setting right outside the window making it difficult to see clearly. "Who is it?" he asked.

"Not sure." She walked out of the room, and Cole followed. He finally caught up to her as she stepped out on the back porch just in time to recognize the deputy sheriff getting out of the patrol car along with another man.

Cole stood close enough to feel her tense.

The man in the khaki uniform tipped his hat. "Good evening, ma'am." He walked toward the porch, but stopped at the base of the steps. "I'm Deputy Clarke."

"Evening, Deputy," Rachel said. "What brings you out here?"

"We're looking for Rachel Hewitt."

"I'm Rachel Hewitt."

The two men exchanged a look, then the deputy asked, "Do you have a sister named Sarah?"

A whimpering sound escaped Rachel, and Cole automatically moved closer. "Yes…" she answered.

"Could we come inside? We'd like to ask you some questions."

Rachel nodded and the two men walked up the steps and into the kitchen. "Have you seen my sister? Is she in Fort Stockton?"

"No," the deputy answered. "This is Mike Bentley. He's from social services in San Antonio. That's where your sister has been living for the past few months."

Suddenly the back door opened and Cy walked in. "Rachel…why is the sheriff's car…?"

"Cy, these gentlemen are here about Sarah. She's been living in San Antonio."

Cy and Cole exchanged a worried look. The sheriff didn't show up on your doorstep with good news. "Is that a fact?"

The man from social services finally spoke. "We tried to find her family, but it wasn't until a friend came looking for her that we knew about you, Ms. Hewitt."

"Er, maybe you should sit down, ma'am," the deputy said.

Rachel blinked. "Is my sister in trouble, Deputy?"

He shook his head. "I'm sorry to say Sarah died nearly three weeks ago in an automobile accident."

Rachel didn't hear much more as the buzzing in her head drowned out everything else but the words,

*Sarah died.* She felt herself sinking, until Cole put his arm around her and held her up.

"I've got you," he whispered. "Just lean on me."

Struggling to regain her composure, Rachel straightened. "Please, sit down." She moved around the kitchen. "I'll make some coffee."

She suddenly felt Cole grip her trembling hands and stop her. "Rachel, we don't need coffee. You need to sit down." His eyes held hers. "Do you want me to call someone?"

She shook her head. "Just…can you…stay with me?"

"Of course." He led her to the table and sat her down in a chair, then pulled out another one for himself.

"I'm sorry to put you through this, Ms. Hewitt, but your sister didn't leave much information about her family. And it was important we find you because…" The two men exchanged a long look, then the deputy continued, "Because before your sister died she gave birth to a baby girl."

# CHAPTER TWO

AT SIX-THIRTY the next morning, Rachel dressed in a dark skirt and white blouse. The night had passed in a blur. She had relied on Cy and Cole to take the details about her sister's accident. After the words, blown tire, she hadn't processed much more. Later, Rachel learned that Sarah had lost control of her car and crashed into a tree. Her sister had been in a coma when the doctor delivered her baby four weeks prematurely.

Unable to sleep, Rachel had wandered through the house, trying to rid herself of the guilt that threatened to consume her. She should have tried harder to find Sarah, tried harder to bring her home.

Now, she was bringing home her sister's baby daughter.

After packing an overnight bag for the trip to San Antonio, she went out where Cy and Cole were waiting beside the dark late-model truck. Cole took her bag and placed it inside the crew cab. She turned to Cy.

"Are you sure you're well enough to handle things?"

"Shoot, I could do it with my eyes closed." He

hugged her. "To ease your mind, Bud Campbell is stopping by to help out."

Rachel studied the man who'd been the only loving force in her life. He was like an uncle to her. "Just don't overdo it. I left some chicken in the refrigerator for you. So be sure to eat it, and not that fried food and heavy gravy from the diner in town."

"Stop nagging me, girl." Cy hugged her. "You have enough to worry about." He glanced at Cole. "Make sure she eats, too."

"Will do," Cole promised as he opened the door. "We better get on the road."

After Rachel climbed in, he started the engine and headed toward Interstate Ten. Cole tried not to speed, wanting to arrive safely, but it was a long way to San Antonio. For the first few hours Rachel just sat there and stared out the window. The constant steady hum of the engine was the only sound in the truck cab.

"Do you think she suffered?" Rachel finally asked.

Her blunt question caught Cole off guard. He knew all too well how fragile life could be. How fast everything could be snatched away from you. Rachel knew it now, too. "I don't think so. They said she was unconscious when they got to the car."

He glanced out the windshield at the miles of highway ahead of them. He didn't want to think about Rachel's pain. He had no doubt she was feeling the hurt clear through to the bone. She'd lost a sister she hadn't seen in years and that empty ache wasn't going away...not for a long time.

"I used to hate her, you know." Rachel turned to

him. "I was so angry at her for leaving me. And not once did she wonder how I was doing…or how Father was."

"I didn't know your sister, Rachel. But maybe she had her reasons."

"Oh, she had her reasons, all right. She hated the ranch and she hated Father."

"A lot of parents and kids have disagreements," he said, but he knew there was more. He'd heard about Gib Hewitt's reputation. The men who worked for him considered him a tyrant. Apparently he hadn't treated his daughters much better, either.

"Sarah always rebelled. It seemed she did things to purposely anger Father. One day she told me she was going to leave and make a life for herself." Rachel looked away. "She took money from Father's desk."

Cole took his eyes off the road to glance in her direction. "What did your father do?"

"He said that she was just like our mother. That she was no good. He no longer had a daughter named Sarah."

Cole cursed under his breath. "Your father might have been overly strict, Rachel, but Sarah had to know that you loved her."

"All I wanted was for her to come home," Rachel said and he could hear the emotion in her voice. "Now…it's too late."

"It's not too late for her baby. You can bring her daughter back to the Bar H."

But deep in his heart Cole knew too well that not everybody got a second chance.

\* \* \*

Cole hadn't been in a hospital in nearly two years. Not since Jillian had been rushed into emergency. Suddenly he felt light-headed and his body began to tremble. He fought it, but couldn't push away the memories as the antiseptic smell threatened to choke him. There had been many times he'd wished it had. Then he wouldn't have to face the questions, the accusations…the guilt.

For Rachel's sake, he had to pull it together. It had been a long day already and she still needed to meet with the social worker in charge of her niece's case.

Cole punched the button for the elevator and looked at Rachel's pale face. He took her cold hand in his and held it while they rode up to the fourth floor. All too soon the bell chimed and they got off, then walked toward the nurse's station.

"I'm Rachel Hewitt, and I'm here to meet Mrs. Nealey."

The young, blond nurse pointed to the reception area where a middle-aged woman was seated doing paperwork. Rachel went to her. "Mrs. Nealey?"

The woman stood and offered a friendly smile. "Yes, I'm Beth Nealey. You must be Rachel Hewitt."

"How did you know?"

"I saw a picture of you…in your sister's things."

Rachel's eyes widened. "Sarah had a picture of me?"

The social worker nodded. "You were both a lot younger, but it was you." She glanced at Cole. "I'm sure the police will give you the rest of her things now that you've been located."

"My sister and I haven't seen each other in over eight years," Rachel whispered.

As much as he tried to stay back, Cole found himself stepping closer to offer his strength. "Had Sarah always lived in San Antonio?" he asked.

Mrs. Nealey shook her head. "The police and I have recently learned Sarah had been in town for only the past few months." The social worker continued, "She rented a furnished apartment, and paid week to week. She worked as a waitress at a local diner. The car she was driving was registered in a friend's name, Carrie Johnston, who was out of town at the time of the accident. Ms. Johnston returned this week and that's how we learned about you, Ms. Hewitt."

"What about the baby's father?" Rachel asked. "Was Sarah married?"

"We haven't found any record of a marriage license. According to your sister's friend, the baby's father wanted no part of the child's life. If that's so, you're the baby's only known relative."

Thirty minutes and several questions later, Rachel excused herself and walked down the hospital corridor to the restroom. She needed some time to pull herself together. After washing her hands, she splashed cold water on her face. Instead of returning to the waiting area, she ended up in the small hospital chapel and knelt down.

For a while she prayed for the sister she'd missed every day since she'd left home. Then she began to question God as to why he took Sarah away.

A sadness like she'd never known before threatened to overwhelm her as she pictured the once laughing little girl she'd shared so much with. She raised her baby sister after their mother abandoned them. Sarah had followed Rachel around, mimicking her.

But as Sarah had gotten older, she began to rebel, refusing to let Gib Hewitt keep her under his thumb. Rachel had envied Sarah her courage...her courage to leave. That hadn't stopped Rachel's years of wishing Sarah would come back home.

But her sister wasn't coming back. She had to accept that.

Rachel drew a shaky breath. A quiet peace settled within her as she said her final goodbye.

Now she needed to concentrate on making a home for her niece.

Cole watched Rachel as she came down the hall. It was obvious this was taking a toll on her. It hadn't helped him much, either. No matter how hard he fought it his own memories had returned, threatening him with his own painful past, sending him back to the best and the worst times in his life.

He turned his attention to Rachel as she tried to smile, but didn't quite pull it off. He automatically drew her close, reveling in her warm touch seeping into his skin. It could be addicting if he let it.

"I was in the chapel. Was Mrs. Nealey looking for me?"

Cole stepped back. "She came by and asked if you wanted to see the baby."

Rachel's brown eyes grew wide. "Really? But I thought she was still in the neonatal unit."

"She is, but you're allowed in because you're family."

This time her smile made it. "I am, aren't I?"

"So, you ready to go meet your niece?"

Just then Beth Nealey arrived and led them down the hall to the glass window of the nursery. "The baby has been putting on weight for the past two weeks," she said. "She's at six pounds five ounces now. She's taking three ounces of formula per feeding and keeping it down. Of course, the nurses will fill you in on her schedule before you take her home."

*Home. So soon?*

Beth smiled. "I can't tell you how happy we are that we found you—not that this little one would have any trouble finding loving parents, but a blood relative is always our first choice. Have you come up with a name for her?"

Rachel opened her mouth, but had no answer. "No… I haven't thought about that."

"It may help you to know that in your sister's things, she had a baby blanket with the name Hannah Marie embroidered in the corner. But it's up to you."

Rachel nodded.

"Well, then, let's meet your niece." Mrs. Nealey motioned for her to follow.

She looked over her shoulder at Cole.

"I'll wait here for you," he told her.

Rachel hoped he'd go with her, but realized she shouldn't depend on him, especially since he was leaving soon. At this moment she was selfish enough to take what was offered. She went through the door, and after she scrubbed up, was taken into the unit where a nurse removed a bundled baby from the clear plastic incubator, and placed the infant into Rachel's arms.

She looked down at the tiny girl with a full head of dark hair, and scrunched up face, and her breath caught. The baby yawned and opened her eyes. They were the identical color of Sarah's, crystal-blue. Rachel took the infant's hand and when the tiny fingers gripped hers she fell instantly in love.

"I think I've decided on a name for her," she said. "Instead of Hannah Marie, I'm going with Hannah Sarah…after her mother."

"I want to talk with the doctor," Rachel insisted when she came out of the nursery.

"Tomorrow is soon enough," Cole said as he led her to the elevators. "I know you want to stay with the baby, but you need rest, Rachel. When you take the newborn home, you aren't going to get any…for a while anyway. We'll let the doctor know where we're staying. In the meantime let's get something to eat."

An hour later, after a light supper, Cole registered them at the large chain hotel across from the hospital. He carried in the overnight bags they'd thrown together for the trip. They rode the elevator to the third floor, and walked silently down the corridor.

"I've never stayed in a hotel before," Rachel announced. "Father would have thought it was a waste of money."

Cole didn't doubt that was something Hewitt would think. "Well, this isn't the fanciest place around, but it's nice enough." In his travels, he had stayed in more places like this than he wanted to remember. He inserted the key card, showing Rachel how to open the door, then ushered her inside and flipped on a light, revealing two double beds, a dresser, desk and television.

"Oh, this is nice," she said, looking around, and peering into the small bathroom.

Cole tossed her bag on one of the beds. "You'll be comfortable here," he said. "I'll be next door if you need anything." He went to the door that connected the rooms. "Don't hesitate to call me." He prayed she wouldn't. He'd already broken too many of his rules about getting involved as it was.

Rachel felt awkward, shy. Cole Parrish was practically a stranger, and yet she'd never relied on anyone as much as she had this man. And she'd never been in this kind of situation before. Here she was alone with a man in a hotel room. Not that anything was going to happen. Her face suddenly flushed at the thought. But so many things had changed in the last few days. Her life would never be the same.

"I can't thank you enough for all you've done," she said. "Driving me all the way here…staying with me through…everything. I'll pay you back…"

"No problem," he said and opened the door. "Just get some sleep, Rachel." Then he was gone before she could say more.

"You…too," she whispered as the door clicked

closed behind him. She looked around again. Suddenly the silence was oppressive and her feelings rushed to the surface. She collapsed on the bed and finally let go.

In his room, Cole stripped off his clothes and headed for the bathroom. He turned on the tap in the shower, and even before the temperature warmed he stepped in. He wanted the shock of the cold water to make him forget…again. Sticking his head under the spray, he fought back the memories—fought the emotions that threatened to bring him to his knees.

"Not now. I can't," he choked, wanting to remember the child he'd loved, but not wanting the pain that always accompanied the retrospection. But the two couldn't be separated. He couldn't have one without the other.

Cole quickly soaped his body and rinsed, then climbed out of the shower. After dressing in clean underwear and jeans, he walked into the bedroom. He decided some television might be a good distraction. He went to the table for the remote, and lying with his wallet and change, he found the small medallion he'd carried in his pocket for the past months. The tiny St. Christopher's medal that was once pinned in his son's crib, a crib that Nathan never got the chance to sleep in.

The familiar tightness constricted his chest, gripping his heart, making it hard to breathe. He welcomed the physical pain. He deserved it. He rubbed the medal between his fingers. It was a constant reminder of what he'd lost. What he could never bring back.

A faint sound drew Cole's attention. He listened and realized it was Rachel crying in the next room. He told himself it was good she was finally letting go of her pain. He wasn't going to invade her privacy.

Over an hour later, still unable to sleep, he'd gotten engrossed in an action movie, but not so much that he hadn't kept an ear turned to Rachel's room. It had been pretty quiet, and he was grateful she'd fallen asleep.

He had dozed off when he heard the murmured sounds, too loud to ignore. He got up and went to the connecting door, cracked it open and spoke her name.

No answer. He saw her lying on the bed, dressed in a white cotton nightgown that had ridden up, revealing long, gorgeous legs. Desire shot through him and he quickly dragged his gaze to her face as she tossed back and forth on the pillow, crying out. He went to her, and sat down on the edge of the bed.

"Rachel…" he said, but she didn't answer. He finally reached out and touched her shoulder. She jerked up with a gasp.

"Cole," she whispered in a husky voice. Their gazes locked and he wanted to absorb the sadness he saw in those depths.

"You were having a nightmare."

She brushed back her long, wavy hair with a trembling hand. "Oh God, I was dreaming that Sarah came home. She was pregnant, but Father threw her out. I was running after her…begging her not to leave." Her lips quivered as she fought for control.

"Oh, Cole, I can't believe it. She's gone. I'd always hoped she'd come back."

The dim light didn't hide her anguish. "She might have. But it was Sarah's choice, Rachel. She chose to leave and you chose to stay on the ranch. You can't punish yourself for something you didn't have any control over."

She drew a shaky breath. "I wish it could have been different."

"There are things we all wish could be different, but wishing doesn't make it so."

"I never got to tell her I loved her."

Rachel Hewitt was a strong woman, but the past two days would knock the strongest person down. He finally pulled her into his arms and inhaled her soft fragrance.

He wanted desperately to give her strength, but he didn't have any to spare. All he could manage was human contact, which he needed as much as she did. He caressed her back as he pressed a soft kiss on top of her head.

"It's going to be all right," he lied. His hands continued to move over her. The action seemed to calm her. He touched her hair, smoothing it back from her tearstained face.

"You don't know," she said. "Before Sarah left, I said so many awful things to her. I was jealous. She was so pretty. I was just…plain. She had everything and she was leaving me with Father."

"Oh, Rachel, you could never be cruel on purpose and don't ever say you're plain."

She raised her face to his, her eyes wondrous, making his pulse race. Before he knew what he was doing, he bent down and touched his mouth to hers, telling himself it was to reassure and comfort her.

She sucked in a tiny breath as he caressed her lips, tasting her softness, her sweetness. Her fingers raised to his chest and the contact seared his skin. He pulled her against his body and deepened the kiss. His tongue teased the seam of her lips open and Rachel whimpered. More heat surged through him.

It had been so long…so long since he'd wanted anyone, craved any closeness on a physical level. But Rachel was exactly the kind of woman he couldn't get involved with. She wasn't a one-night stand. She'd made him feel…too much. No, he couldn't go through that again. He broke off the kiss and saw her eyes glazed with desire.

"Cole…" She spoke his name so intimately, as if they'd already been lovers.

He shivered and fought to keep his body in control. "I'm sorry, I shouldn't have done that. I was out of line." He started to get up, but she refused to let him go.

"Please," she whispered, "don't leave me."

Cole froze. He had to get out of there, but seeing Rachel's panic, he couldn't move. He of all people knew what it was like to need someone.

Without a word, he drew the blanket over her, then he laid on top and cradled her against him. He held her until he felt her go slack in his arms. She had fallen asleep. He smiled, then eased her off his chest.

He started to lay her down on the bed when she tightened her hold.

"Please…stay," she whispered, sleepily. "Just for a little while."

He bit back a groan. "Okay, Rachel… I won't leave you," he murmured, then stretched out next to her and drew her to his side, her head resting against his shoulder. Maybe together, holding each other, they could keep the demons at bay. For a short time anyway.

# CHAPTER THREE

RACHEL came awake slowly. Her head hurt as if she'd been hit between the eyes. Then the memories of last night slowly started coming back to her. The news of Sarah's death, the trip to San Antonio, her niece, Cole's kiss, his holding her in his arms…

She blinked, and opened her eyes to find the man asleep beside her in bed. Not just beside her, but with his hand draped over her… She froze, and forced herself to breathe as her skin under his palm began to tingle. Her heart started to race.

*Oh my, what do I do?*

She lay motionless and listened to Cole's soft snores. He didn't seem to be too bothered by the situation. Maybe he was used to waking up with a woman. Of course he had, Cole was a good-looking man.

Rachel had never woken up next to a man. She'd dreamed of someone like Cole Parrish coming into her solitary life. But she'd never be the kind of woman who could make him stay.

She closed her eyes, reveling in the feel of his

strong arms around her, but knew she couldn't keep depending on this man. He'd done so much to help her already. Neither one of them needed to add to this already complicated situation.

She tried to slip toward the edge of the bed to get away. It didn't work. Cole murmured something incoherent and pulled her closer, tucking his nearly naked body behind hers.

She bit back a gasp, unable to ignore the sudden warmth that shot through her. Then, as if that weren't enough, his hand began to move under the sheet, first over her stomach, then down to her hips and back up again, returning to her breasts, sending tingles over her skin as his fingers gently pinched her nipple. She closed her eyes, lost in the sudden pleasure. Heaven help her, she wanted to know what it felt like to be caressed by this man, but her common sense finally returned and she pushed his hand away.

"Cole," she murmured his name and sat up.

"What?" He jerked up into a sitting position, rubbed his eyes and looked at her. "Rachel? Oh God." He shot off the bed as if it had caught fire. "Please tell me I didn't do anything—"

"No," she quickly interrupted him. "Absolutely not."

He looked relieved and that disappointed her. "I'm so sorry," he began. "I meant to leave after you fell asleep, but I guess I drifted off…"

"I think we were both pretty tired…" she said, filling her gaze with unbelievably broad shoulders, a naked chest covered with a dusting of dark hair that swirled down his flat stomach and dipped into the open button on his jeans. Her attention quickly moved up to his face.

He started to pace. "That doesn't give me the right to take advantage."

"You didn't," she insisted. "Now, let's stop talking about it." Rachel stood, then quickly realized she had on her nightgown. "We should go back to the hospital."

Their gazes locked, his silver gaze had a sexy sleepy look. "I'll be ready in fifteen," he said.

She glanced away. "I need to shower."

He nodded. "Just knock on the door when you're ready to go. We'll have some breakfast, then head to the hospital."

He walked through the connecting door and shut it behind him. Rachel let out a breath and wondered if she'd ever be able to look at Cole, and not think about his kiss…his touch.

He'd kissed her. The one and only other time she'd been kissed, she'd been thirteen and Billy Michaels nearly chickened out. With the less than satisfying end result, she'd wished he had. Rachel never got another chance to repeat the experience. Her father refused to allow any boys out to the ranch. Later on she'd never had the time to even think about a man in her life.

Cole Parrish was different. From the first time he'd arrived at the Bar H, he'd made her feel things. With one glance, one piercing look, her body came alive. And his kiss last night made her desire things… womanly things.

She shook her head, and walked into the bathroom. She didn't have the time to think about a man in her life.

Now all she had time to think about was making a go of the ranch, and making a home for her niece. The thought of little Hannah Sarah Hewitt brought a wistful smile to her face. She had a family now.

"Just keep supporting her head," the nurse instructed.

"Oh…she's so tiny," Rachel said, gazing down at the tiny bundle in her arms.

Cindy, the pediatric nurse, grinned. "They grow pretty fast. Your niece here has already taken her first bottle this morning. And by those sucking sounds, I'd say she's ready again." Cindy led Rachel to the rocking chair. "Get comfortable."

Nervous, Rachel did as she was told. She didn't have any experience with babies. Not unless you counted calves. "What if…?"

"Stop worrying. Babies are pretty sturdy. And this one has proven that. She's a toughie. We nicknamed her 'Champ.'"

"Well, I hope you're not too upset if I call her Hannah." Rachel smiled as she brought the nipple to her niece's rosebud mouth. The baby took it in and began to suck. "She's drinking."

"That's the plan," the nurse said as she stood by watching, then showed Rachel how to burp Hannah.

Through it all, the infant seemed to survive Rachel's inexperience, and in the end, she fell asleep.

"Since I'm not needed anymore, I'll leave you

two." Before the nurse departed, she motioned to the window. "You know, your husband can come in if he wants, just so long as he puts on a gown."

Rachel glanced around to find Cole standing behind the glass. "Oh, we're not married. Cole works on my ranch."

"Well, whatever. But that's one good-looking cowboy." Cindy sighed. "And it seems to me, he's pretty attentive for *just* a ranch hand.

Cole waited outside the window. He tried to ignore the sound of the infants in the nursery, but he was drawn to watching them as they waved their arms and cried for attention. Their lung power was incredible.

Nathan hadn't been that lucky. His lungs hadn't developed enough… The pain hit Cole hard and he turned away. For so long he kept busy so he wouldn't remember, but the memory of his stillborn son was always there. He had to get away from here.

A nurse came by. "Could you tell Rachel Hewitt that I'll be back in an hour?" he asked her.

When she agreed, he headed for the elevators. There were several details he had to take care of before they could go back to the ranch. He mostly needed some fresh air and to clear his head.

But he knew nothing would ever heal his heart.

The doctor told Rachel he would release Hannah from the hospital in the morning. Was she ready to handle a newborn on her own? She glanced around for Cole but didn't see him anywhere.

When the nurse had given her his message, she wasn't surprised that he needed time alone. He'd had to wait around the hospital most of yesterday and all morning. Who wouldn't want some fresh air? But his disappearance still bothered her. He'd been by her side the entire time. Even though she told herself not to depend on him, she had.

"Don't get used to it, girl, he's not going to be around much longer," she murmured to herself.

Rachel realized that except for Cy, Cole was the only man she'd been able to depend on. And he'd be leaving—at the end of the week.

For the past hour, Rachel had stayed busy with the baby. The police officer who'd handled Sarah's case came by to have her sign papers for her sister's personal things, and to explain the landlord had the rest of Sarah's clothes.

Then Beth Nealey arrived and invited her to lunch in the cafeteria. After they went through the food line, they sat down at a table and began to eat. "As far as we discovered in our investigation, you are Hannah's only living relative. So unless you've had a change of heart, you'll be her guardian."

Excitement and fear raced through Rachel as she tried to eat her tomato soup. Once again she thought about Cole, wanting him with her. "No, I haven't changed my mind. Hannah is my niece. I love her already and I want to make a home for her. When possible, I want to adopt her."

Beth smiled, putting Rachel at ease. "I'm glad." She took a bite of her sandwich. "Not to say becoming an instant mother isn't going to be difficult, especially with running a cattle ranch."

"I have help." She could handle this. She wanted Hannah so much she was willing to do anything. "I may be new at motherhood, but I'm willing to do whatever it takes. If I can't handle both, I'll sell the ranch."

Beth patted her hand. "You'll make a great mother, Rachel." She placed her napkin on her tray. "And I'll be coming by in a few weeks to see how things are going. And if you need anything before then, you can always call me."

"So I can take Hannah home tomorrow?"

"Yes. I'll have the papers to sign tomorrow morning before she is released." Beth shook Rachel's hand and stood. "I wish you all the best." With a parting smile, Rachel watched her walk away.

At the door to the cafeteria, Beth stopped when Cole appeared. After a minute they shook hands and Cole came toward Rachel, noticing the other women in the room were giving him an extra long look. She felt her heart speed up as his gaze searched for hers.

He smiled as she reached her table. "I just heard the good news," he told her as he pulled out a chair.

She nodded. "I guess we have to stay one more night," Rachel said. "I'm sorry. This wasn't exactly in your job description."

Cole knew that neither one of them had thought about what was going to happen once they came to San Antonio.

"It's a slow time at the ranch," he assured her with a shrug. Even if Cy was so crippled with arthritis that he could barely get up some mornings, he should be able to handle things while they were gone. "I called Cy while you were in with the baby. He said Bud had been by to help out."

Rachel blinked in surprise. "I'm glad. Cy has trouble asking for help. And since the heart attack, I worry about him overdoing things. And after you leave…" She paused. "I'm sorry, I know you have another job to go to."

He nodded. "If you need me to, I don't have a problem staying on another week. I'll work at finding you another hand." He knew staying on would be tough but how could he leave her alone with a new baby?

"I can't ask you to do that."

"You didn't, Rachel. I offered. Things have changed and you've got to concentrate on the baby for now, not the ranch."

She blinked. "I appreciate it. More than you know. I was worried about what my lawyer was going to say about Hannah." She shrugged. "It shouldn't matter since I'm to take over control of the ranch in a few weeks."

He smiled again. "I hear you're having a special birthday."

"The only thing that's good about it is I can run the ranch my way without having to ask Mr. Montgomery."

He nodded. "You have a lot on your plate. Top of the list is collecting your sister's things. Mrs. Nealey told me that the police stopped by." He glanced down at the bag on the chair. "How about we take care of that now?"

Rachel started to argue, then realized she had no other way to get Sarah's things. "Thank you, Cole. I'd appreciate that."

"Easier today than tomorrow when you have the baby."

Together, they walked out of the hospital into the bright summer sun and across the parking lot to his truck. He helped Rachel into her seat. As he walked around the driver's side, Rachel noticed several boxes and packages filled the backseat. There was a box that was labeled, a baby carrier. Several packages of newborn-size disposable diapers. A case of formula.

He opened his door and climbed in.

"Cole, what's all this?"

He tossed a glance to the rear of the truck. "Things the baby will need when we get back to the ranch."

She hadn't even thought that far ahead, but obviously he had. "You bought it all?"

"Believe me, it's not all you'll need. Like clothes, but I figured you'd want to pick those out yourself." He shrugged as he put the key in the ignition.

"Cole...how did you know what to buy?"

He stared at her for a long time, then finally said, "I almost had a son."

Cole had a son?

Two hours later, even distracted with the trip to Sarah's landlord to pick up her things, which consisted of two suitcases and three boxes, Rachel could still hear the echo of Cole's words. *A son.*

Was Cole Parrish also married? She thought about

their kiss last night. She glanced across the front seat. Of course someone as handsome as Cole would have a woman who loved him. For the first time in her life she'd felt desired. Felt like a woman.

Suddenly Cole braked the truck and turned the corner. The tires squealed and Rachel grabbed the seat.

"Cole, what's wrong?"

He pulled up to the curb and threw the gearshift into Park, then turned to her. "I don't know, Rachel. Why don't you tell me? For the past hour you've acted like I've grown two heads. If it's about last night, I've already apologized…"

"I know. And that wasn't all your fault anyway. I was the one who asked you not to leave…"

His deep gaze held hers, making it hard to breathe.

"It's just what you said…about your son."

She saw the pain etched on his face and she wanted to take back the words.

"I was never a father. I never got the chance. My son was born premature. He didn't survive…and neither did my marriage."

"Oh, Cole." She didn't know what to say to comfort him. Instead she reached out and touched his arm. She felt him tense, but he didn't pull away. "I'm sorry. The past few days must have been rough for you, having to relive…everything."

He stared at her hand. "It hasn't exactly been a picnic for you, either."

She nodded. "And you've been there for me." She thought back to when Cole held her, kissed her. "I want to be there for you…"

Cole gasped air into his starved lungs, and fought to keep from reaching for her, from burying himself in her softness…in the comfort she was offering. "Be careful, Rachel. We're both vulnerable right now. And I'm not the guy who's going to make you promises…" He couldn't anymore. "When the time comes, I'm still going to leave."

"I'm not asking you for any promises."

Cole studied her luminous brown eyes and felt the ice chipping away from his heart. He leaned forward, catching her unique scent. The clean…innocent sweetness that was suddenly becoming as intoxicating as a drug.

All he wanted to do was pull her across the seat and into his arms, feel her melt against him as his mouth devoured hers until they both had enough. Problem was he knew he'd never get enough of her.

"You deserve it all, Rachel." He glanced out the window at the traffic passing by. "Just not with someone like me…a drifter."

Her chin came up. "I don't need a man to give me a home, Cole. My concern right now is raising my niece. It's just I know what it's like to be alone…" Her voice had such compassion. "Soon, I inherit the ranch…and have control of the finances. I'd be able to pay you a little more—that is if you decide you want to stay."

For the first time in a long time, Cole wanted what she offered. "I already said I'd stay on a few weeks until we find you someone else. But then I have to leave. Believe me, Rachel, it's better this way…for everyone. Sooner or later, I'd end up letting you down. All I can offer you is a few weeks."

She started to speak, but hesitated. "Then I'll take it, Cole. And thank you for all your help getting my sister's things." She brightened. "And for shopping for all the baby things."

He smiled. "That was easy. Caring for a newborn around the clock will be the hard part."

The next morning about 10:00 a.m., Rachel had officially become her niece's guardian. She would start adoption proceedings as soon as possible, but for now, she would take her home. It wasn't the way she'd planned motherhood to happen to her, but she already loved this baby.

That was what she'd promised Sarah as she stood at the unmarked grave with Hannah asleep in the carrier beside her. Cole had placed an azalea plant with bright pink blossoms on the freshly mown grass, then quietly disappeared, giving Rachel privacy to say goodbye to her sister.

In the end, Rachel made several promises to her sibling, most importantly, to love and raise Hannah as her own child. She brushed away the tears, picked up the baby and walked to the truck...to Cole.

Back on the road, they'd driven until Hannah needed to be fed and changed again, then grabbed a couple of hamburgers at a drive-through restaurant, and ate on the way home.

Luckily Hannah slept most of the way. The soft country music on the radio helped swallow the miles that stretched ahead of them. They'd kept the conversation from getting personal, just ranch business. Finally by early evening they arrived at the Bar H.

Rachel had never loved her home as much as she did at this moment. Even with the run-down appearance, the barn was faded red and the outbuildings needed a whitewashing, too, but the structures were solid. She smiled seeing her vegetable garden at the side of the house, and the colorful pansies she'd planted around the porch.

This was where she belonged...and now, so did Hannah.

Cole parked at the back door of the house. "We're here."

"Yes, we are. And just in time," she said as she glanced back at Hannah. She was waking up. "She needs to be fed."

"Then you take her inside, and Cy and I will bring in everything else."

Rachel nodded toward the foreman who had just come out on the porch and was walking down the steps. He hugged her. "Welcome home."

Rachel smiled. "It's good to be back." Just then a tiny cry came from the backseat.

"Looks like our new resident is making her presence known."

Rachel opened the back door and unfastened the carrier. "Better get used to it. Hannah isn't shy about letting us know when she needs something."

"Well, then bring the young'un inside so I can get a good look at her."

Rachel walked into the kitchen with the scarred cabinets, old appliances and even the worn flooring, which didn't seem so bad after all. She was also happy to see the Crock-Pot of stew on the counter.

"Mary sent over dinner with Bud when he came and helped with chores."

"That was so nice of her." She didn't have to worry about cooking supper. Hannah's cries grew more insistent. Cy ambled over to comfort her, but she was having none of it. Her feet and arms pumped in the air.

Cole came through the door with the diaper bag. "Thank you," she said, and took out a bottle already measured and mixed. She turned on the tap. "Here, Cy, hold this under the spray while I change her."

Rachel grabbed a diaper and wipes, then lifted the baby out and went into the living room. The sofa would do as a changing table for now. She had just finished the quick diaper change when Cole arrived with the warmed bottle.

She cradled Hannah in her arms and placed the bottle in her mouth. Silence.

"My, she sure can make a lot of racket for such a little thing," Cy said as he took the seat across from her.

"Hopefully, when I get her on a schedule, it'll get better." Rachel prayed it would, but she wasn't sure she knew what she was doing, either.

"And her own room," Cy said with a smile. "Bud helped me bring down your old baby bed from the attic. We put it in the room across from yours. And Mary brought over some baby clothes."

She was touched. "Thank you, Cy. That was so

sweet of all of you." Rachel set the bottle down, raised Hannah to her shoulder and patted gently.

"You're welcome. We all need to pitch in. Oh, and there's also a basket kind-of-bed…"

"A bassinet," Cole said.

"That's it." The foreman eyed him. "How did you know?"

Before Cole could speak, Rachel jumped in. "We both learned more about babies than I thought possible. While I was at the hospital, Cole did some shopping for Hannah, too."

Cy drew up a bushy eyebrow. "Well, isn't that nice of you."

"A baby needs a lot of things." Cole moved to the door. "Come on, Cy, you can help me bring it all inside."

Rachel smiled as she listened to the two men grumble at each other as they walked out. She glanced down at her sleeping niece. "Welcome home, Hannah. Welcome home."

Cole never minded living in a bunkhouse. He'd been in several over the last eighteen months, and the Bar H accommodations were better than most ranches.

He had a small room that he'd been staying in for the past months that had been adequate and fairly comfortable. That was until he'd spent the night holding Rachel in his arms.

Cole cursed as he climbed out of his single bunk and pulled on his jeans. He knew it was after midnight, but he couldn't sleep. Standing at the window, he looked toward the house. He saw a soft light coming from the second floor window and figured Rachel was up feeding the baby.

In the stillness, he heard the baby's lusty cries, then saw the silhouette of Rachel holding Hannah against her shoulder as she paced back and forth.

Hannah Hewitt was one feisty kid. He smiled, trying to hold off his own pain as "what if" memories filled his head. The baby's cries grew more intense and Cole wondered if something was wrong. He shook his head. He didn't have any firsthand experience with babies, and neither did Rachel. The twosome passed by the window once again and Cole began to suspect maybe something else could be wrong. He pulled on a pair of boots, grabbed his shirt from the chair and headed across the yard to the house.

Upstairs, Rachel fought her panic, but nothing she did would stop Hannah's cries. She just stiffened up her little body and wailed…and wailed. She paced and rocked trying to soothe the baby, but nothing worked.

Suddenly she heard her name. It was Cole.

"Rachel, can I come in?" he called again from the hall.

"Please…" She sighed as he appeared in the doorway, in jeans and a shirt that he hadn't taken the time to button.

"Oh, Cole, I can't get her to stop crying. I think there's something wrong. Maybe I did something wrong. I don't know anymore."

Without hesitation, Cole crossed the room and took Hannah from her. He placed the screaming infant against his bare chest. With a voice that was soft and low, he stroked her back up and down as he swayed back and forth. After a few moments there was a hearty burp that brought a smile to Cole's mouth.

"That should make her feel better."

Rachel was amazed. "Why wouldn't she do that for me?"

"I think eventually she would have."

Little Hannah shifted on his chest and settled into a sound sleep. "Will you look at that? She must have had an air bubble or something."

"I need to get a book." She combed her hand through her hair and crossed her arms over her thin nightgown. Suddenly self-conscious, she stole a glance at Cole with his mussed hair and rumpled shirt.

The image of the two of them together at the hotel rushed into her head. What surprised her was the feeling of intimacy she felt with him holding a baby in his arms.

"Where do you want me to put her?"

She blinked. "Oh, what?"

"The baby. Do you want her in the crib?"

"Yes, please."

Cole gently laid the sleeping baby on the sheet and stood back as Rachel tucked a light blanket over her. He should just leave, but he couldn't seem to stop watching Rachel with the baby. As much as he'd tried to stay detached from Hannah, when he held her, it was as if she reached her tiny hand into his chest and grabbed hold of his heart. He worked to draw air into his lungs and he looked at Rachel.

She was trouble, too.

"Do you think she'll sleep the rest of the night?"

He shrugged, knowing she was a little frightened to be alone with the baby. He wasn't about to help her out. "Maybe, but you should get some sleep while you have the chance."

Rachel nodded, but didn't move, then finally said, "Thank you again for your help, Cole."

"No problem. And remember, you just worry about taking care of the baby. Cy and I'll handle the stock."

"I hate to impose so much."

"You're not. It's my job. Good night, Rachel." He turned away and made his escape. It would be too easy to stay and let her lean on him. He'd always been that kind of guy, but not anymore. Not since he let down the two most important people in his life. And that was something he could never forgive himself for.

## CHAPTER FOUR

IT HAD been a long first night for Rachel, starting when Hannah stirred about 4:00 a.m. Rachel had been able to settle her this time but she'd been kept awake for a different reason.

*Cole.*

Rachel hadn't been able to blank out the image of him holding Hannah. His large, sure hands cradling the tiny infant against his chest, soothing her, comforting her.

Finally at dawn, Rachel took advantage of the still sleeping infant, showered and dressed in her usual jeans and shirt and braided her long hair. But it was going to be anything but a usual day.

Carefully lifting the baby from the bed to the carrier, she brought her downstairs to start breakfast.

Hannah opened her eyes and Rachel smiled. "Looks like you're going to have to sit and watch me cook. Yes, you are."

The baby waved her hands in the air and made a cooing sound. Something suddenly happened inside

Rachel. Emotions so strong welled in her chest and tears filled her eyes. This little baby was her niece, her family. "Oh, Sarah, you should be here with your little girl."

Rachel gave herself a moment to mourn her sister, but needed to turn her mind to other things. Placing the carrier safely out of the way, she got busy preparing breakfast. By the time she'd put biscuits in the oven, Cy came through the back door. Grumbling, he set a basket of fresh eggs from the henhouse on the counter.

"I'd rather muck out stalls all day long than collect eggs. And one day I'm gonna get pleasure ringin' a few of those birds' necks."

Rachel bit back a smile. "It would be a lot easier if you just used a little sweetness, Cy."

He examined his wounds. "It would be a waste of time on those old hens."

Rachel looked over his hand. "It's not as bad as the last time."

Suddenly Hannah made her presence known and Cy looked over at the carrier. "Will you look here?" The old man smiled. "Well, aren't you all bright-eyed this morning?"

Rachel laughed. "Where was that sweet disposition last night, huh?"

He glanced at Rachel. "How'd it go?"

"Not too bad. Once I got her asleep, she woke up once."

"You've been up since then?"

"I dozed a little." She busied herself cracking the

eggs on the side of the bowl. "Until six. But I feel like I'm fumbling around. Last night she was crying her eyes out. If it wasn't for Cole showing up, I don't know what I would have done."

The foreman raised an eyebrow. "Seems Cole is a pretty handy guy to have around."

Rachel glanced at the content-looking baby. She wasn't going to let Cy's teasing get to her. "He was last night. I can't believe you didn't hear Hannah's ruckus. I thought I'd done something wrong. Cole arrived and settled her down just as easy as you please." She frowned at Cy. "What if I'm not cut out to be a mother?"

"After one night, you're ready to give up? That doesn't sound like you."

"I'm not giving up." She straightened. "It's just that I haven't had any time to adjust to having a baby around. What if I do it wrong?"

"Naw, that's impossible, Rachel. I've seen you nurse foals and calves since you were a kid. You were born for this." The old man sighed and he placed his hand on her arm. "Besides, I think Sarah is happy that you'll be raising her child."

The familiar sadness came over her. In having Hannah, she couldn't forget that she'd also lost her sister. "It sounds funny, Cy, but I miss her." She blinked back tears. "I wanted so much for another chance to be a sister. Just as soon as I inherited the ranch, I was planning to hire an investigator to find her. I guess I'm a few weeks too late."

"We all have a lot of wishes we can't have, darlin'."

He pulled her into his arms. "You've lost a lot of people in your life, but you have this beautiful baby…and me. I couldn't love you more if you were my own."

Rachel wiped away a tear. "I love you, too, Cy. And this precious little girl." She couldn't tell him how much she longed for the kind of love only a man could give her. Her thoughts turned to Cole. Even knowing she wasn't ever going to have a man like him in her life, it didn't stop her wanting.

"You two are the best family a girl could have."

Cy huffed. "I doubt that, but you're stuck with me."

"And I can't think of anyone else I want to be stuck with." She gave him a hug just as the screen door opened and Cole stepped into the room.

Rachel couldn't help but stare, finding she'd been looking forward to seeing him. He was the type of man who drew attention, not just for his good looks but his presence. He wasn't your typical ranch drifter. And over the past few days, she'd learned a lot about the man. That he'd loved someone, and had to suffer the cruel experience of losing a child…his marriage breaking up.

"Morning." He removed his hat, hung it on the hook and came to the table.

"Good morning," Rachel returned and busied herself at the stove. "Breakfast is almost ready."

"No hurry." He glanced at the carrier. "I can wait." He looked down at the baby who quickly became engrossed in him. "How'd she do the rest of the night?" he asked as little Hannah stared back at him with her blue eyes.

Rachel smiled. "She was up at four and I fed her and she went right back to sleep."

As if on cue, Hannah started fussing and Rachel went to her. "I guess she's hungry again."

The cries grew louder and Cole's mouth twitched in amusement. "I think that's what she's trying to tell you."

Rachel picked up the baby, he went to the refrigerator, took out a bottle and put it in the bottle warmer. "You might want to invest in a microwave, it'll heat faster."

Rachel rocked Hannah until finally Cole brought her the warm bottle.

Turning away from the cozy scene, Cole walked to the stove and took over cooking the eggs. He could handle the extra chores, but he didn't want to be pulled any further into this family.

"Thanks, Cole," Rachel began, "for helping with Hannah and with breakfast. I'll try to be more organized tomorrow."

"The baby comes first. I think Cy and I can stumble around for a while." He scooped the eggs onto the plates and carried them to the table, then went back for the bacon and biscuits.

Cy brought the coffee and sat down. "Yeah, Rachel, we can handle things for a while. This morning we're going to move Old Brutus into the south pasture. We should be back by early afternoon, unless you need us here."

"Now, coaxing that stubborn bull to move isn't something I'm going to miss." She glanced down at the baby to see she'd drunk half of the bottle. "We should be fine." She glanced at Cole. "And you have your cell phone, so I can call if anything comes up."

He nodded as a loud knock sounded at the back door.

"Who could that be?" Cy asked.

"Maybe we should find out." Cole walked through the mudroom to find a tall, thin teenage boy standing on the porch.

"Can I help you?"

"I hear you're hiring a ranch hand."

After a closer look at this kid, Cole realized he was barely old enough to shave. His dark blond hair hung past his collar. "Yes, we're looking for a hand."

"I want to apply."

"It's a full-time job, and you'll be in school."

The kid's blue eyes seemed too large for his face. "It's summertime and I don't go to school anymore. I just need a job."

Suddenly Rachel appeared. "Cole, who is it?"

The boy nodded. "Josh Owens, ma'am. I'm here to apply for the job."

Rachel exchanged a glance with Cole. "Well, you are the first to apply, Josh. I'm Rachel Hewitt and this here is Cole Parrish." She stepped aside. "Why don't you come in so we can talk?" The boy looked at Cole, then with his nod, he stepped into the kitchen.

"This is Cy Parks. He's the foreman. Cy, this is Josh Owens."

Cy nodded.

"We're just about to have breakfast," Rachel said. "Why don't you join us?"

Josh played with the battered cowboy hat in his hands. "I don't want to intrude, Miss Hewitt."

"You aren't." She went to the cupboard and took down another plate. "You can wash up in the sink."

"Owens…" Cy began. "Doesn't your family rent the place on the Driscoll property?"

The boy nodded as he used the soap at the sink. "Yes, sir. But my daddy has gone off to find work in Midland. It's just me."

"You're by yourself?" Rachel asked.

"It's okay, ma'am. I've been on my own before." He took an empty seat at the big table. When Rachel set a plate of food in front of him, Josh looked as if it were Christmas morning.

Damn. It was obvious that he had been left to fend for himself, and Cole had known firsthand how that was. He sat down next to the kid.

"Do you have experience working on a ranch?"

"Yes, sir. I worked last summer with my dad." The boy waited until everyone was seated before he began to eat.

Cole caught Rachel's gaze. She also realized the boy's situation. She asked several questions of Josh, then looked at Cole. There was no way she couldn't hire this boy.

"Even if we want to give you the job, Josh, you're underage. We need to get a parent's permission."

Josh's bright eyes quickly dimmed. "I'm not sure

exactly where my dad is…and my mom's been gone for about three years."

Cole had no doubt Josh had been on his own since his mother's absence. By the looks of his overly thin frame, Josh hadn't been eating regularly.

Rachel spoke up. "You know, Cole, we have plenty of room in the bunkhouse for Josh to stay…until we locate his father, that is." She paused. "I could call Beth Nealey and see if she can help find him."

Cole knew it was useless to argue, and he'd be more surprised if she did turn the kid away. "I guess we can give you a try."

Josh stopped eating. "Really? Thank you, sir."

"Stop with the sir. I'm Cole, and this is Cy and Rachel. The baby sleeping in the carrier is Hannah."

He nodded. "Thank you, sir—Cole. You won't be sorry. I'll work hard."

"Since it's summer, you'll be able to work full-time, but if you're around in September, you'll be back in school. You'll have to do chores in the early morning and late afternoon."

Josh glanced around the table. "I don't need to go to school."

"You will if you want to work here. We'll give you a bunk, but you also need your high school diploma. Take it or leave it."

"I'll take it."

"Okay, you can move your things in anytime."

"They're just outside." Josh looked at Rachel. "If it's okay, ma'am, I'd be beholden to you if I could wash up some clothes."

She smiled. "I'll show you how to use the machine after breakfast. Welcome to the Bar H, Josh."

Twenty minutes later, they finished breakfast and Cy took Josh out to the bunkhouse to show him around. Cole hung around to clear away the dishes.

"You know this situation could be a lot of trouble for you," he told her. "You'll be taking responsibility for another kid…"

Rachel only stared at him. Who was the man trying to fool? "And you would turn him away?"

He ignored her question. "I'd call foster care."

"And he'd have to go into a group home. Josh is better off here, Cole. At least he can do my share of work. He's a good kid."

"And you think that because he called you ma'am?"

"No, I could see it in his eyes. He wants to belong. We have to give him a chance, Cole."

"Just call Mrs. Nealey," he told her.

She nodded. "I will today. I can't believe a father would just up and leave his son."

"There are a lot of kids out there like Josh." Cole's steel-gray gaze gave away no secrets from his past, but she had no doubt that he'd been one of those kids. "And it looks like you've just taken responsibility for a seventeen-year-old boy. Seems your family is growing."

By three in the afternoon, Rachel was bored. Since she hadn't had any ranch chores to do, and was confined to the house she'd finished her work a while ago.

By noon she'd bathed Hannah and put her down

for a nap, then set to cleaning the house while doing some laundry. With the baby monitor in hand, Rachel walked into her father's office.

She would take over running the ranch on her own in less than two weeks, and needed to have a direction. This was the first opportunity she'd had since bringing Hannah home to think about business.

The letter from the 21st Century Windmill Company was still on the desk where she had left it. It was time to call and find out more. She dialed the number and waited until someone answered.

Rachel glanced at the name on the letter. "Mr. Douglas Wills, please."

"This is Doug Wills."

"Hello, Mr. Wills. My name is Rachel Hewitt from the Bar H Ranch." She paused. "You sent a letter a few months ago about leasing my land on Rocky Ridge Mesa. Are you still interested?"

"Yes, we are, Miss Hewitt," he said assuredly. "Although I got the impression from Mr. Montgomery that you weren't interested in the project."

Rachel's temper flared. How dare Monty do this without at least talking to her about it? "Mr. Montgomery will no longer be speaking on my behalf. By the end of the month I will be the sole owner of the ranch and I'll be making all decisions. And I'm very much interested in hearing what you have to say."

The conversation proved to be very successful— not only was Mr. Wills coming to visit the ranch, but for the first time Rachel had felt like she was in control. But just then a tiny sound came from the monitor, drawing her attention. She stood and headed for the stairs and her child. All her choices now wouldn't just affect her, but Hannah.

With Cole leaving soon, she had only Cy and herself to depend on. She finally admitted that scared her.

"You know next week is Rachel's birthday. I think we should throw her a party."

Cy had been talking nonstop since they'd saddled up that morning. Even Josh hadn't been able to get a word in, but the kid had kept busy, repairing the downed fence. Not having to be told twice what to do, Josh had let them know for the past two days how grateful he was to have a job. And with Beth Nealey's help, it looked like the boy got to stay…for a while.

"You hearing me?"

"What?" Cole asked as he watched Josh riding up ahead on Rachel's gray mare, Stormy.

"I said Rachel's birthday is the twenty-fourth of the month, next Friday. I know women don't like the idea of turning thirty, but this is a special day for Rachel. She's finally going to be able to have this place all to herself. And without that shyster lawyer to boss her around."

The few times Cole had seen Montgomery at the ranch, he hadn't been impressed with him, either. "Has he been doing anything illegal?"

"I can't prove it, but that doesn't mean I trust the man. The only interest he has is looking out for his own." He shook his head. "Rachel had to beg for every nickel."

Cole watched the small herd of mixed Herefords grazing in the pasture. "Maybe she should sell."

"She loves this place. Of course, it might be an easier life for her if she did, especially now that she has the baby." Cy adjusted his hat as they walked the horses over the rise. "I can't see Rachel living in town."

Cole couldn't, either. He also knew she needed to supplement the Bar H's small cattle operation. "It's a tough life."

"Yeah," the foreman said. "But not so bad if you have someone to share it with."

"She has Hannah."

The old man glared at him. "That's not what I meant. Someone like Rachel has so much love to give. She needs someone who will treat her special. To love her like a woman."

Cole had believed in love once. He'd had it all. A wife and a baby on the way... But he was more worried about making the almighty dollar.

He tugged the horse's reins and headed toward the barn as his thoughts went to his one-time wife, Jillian, and the son he never got to know. He thought about all the mistakes he'd made and how badly things ended. Maybe he was never cut out for family life in the first place. He'd fought through a bad childhood and built a successful business, but he'd lost focus on what was important. His finger traced the medal in his front jeans pocket.

Now, it was too late to get that life back.

"Looks like Rachel has company," Cy said as the house came into view. "I wonder if it's 'good old Monty.'"

As they drew closer, Cole could see the name on the side of the truck was 21$^{st}$ Century Windmill Company. So Rachel had called them.

Cy climbed down from his gelding. "Maybe we should go and see who's here."

Cole dismounted, too, but never took his gaze off the house. "I think Rachel can handle things. If she wants us there, she'll let us know."

Just then the back door opened and a tall man stepped out onto the porch. He was about thirty-something and dressed in dark trousers and a white shirt. He was followed out by Rachel, wearing a long dark skirt and pink blouse. The man leaned forward and said something to her. They both laughed.

"Well, will you look at that." Cy put his hand on his hips. "It seems that someone has taken an interest in our Rachel."

Cole stiffened. So what? Rachel was a pretty woman. "She has that right. But I think this man is here on business."

"And that's the reason he's lingering on the porch, and practically tripping over his tongue when she smiles."

Cole glared and was about to walk his horse into the barn when Rachel looked over and motioned them to come up. Cole and Cy gave their reins to Josh and started for the house. They all met in the yard.

"Oh, Cy and Cole, I'd like you to meet Doug

Wills, from 21$^{st}$ Century. Doug, this is Cy Parks and Cole Parrish."

The men exchanged handshakes.

"Doug's company wants to lease the Rocky Ridge Mesa and plan to construct seventy-five wind turbines."

Doug spoke out. "First, I want Rachel to look over everything before she makes a decision on the project." He turned back to Rachel. "If you have any more questions please call me anytime. My cell phone number is on the back of the card."

"Thank you, I will," Rachel said.

Doug nodded. "Well, I should be going." He took Rachel's hand and shook it, but Cole noticed his touch lingered longer than seemed necessary.

"Bye, Rachel. I hope I'll be hearing from you soon." He nodded to both Cole and Cy, then turned and walked to his truck. They waited until he drove off.

"Well, looks like you've been busy today," Cy said.

Rachel smiled. She'd enjoyed her day and she enjoyed having Doug here. "I'm just thinking ahead." She looked at Cole. "We talked about this before we left for San Antonio. Now that I have Hannah, I need to secure our future. This seemed like a sensible alternative."

Cole opened the door for her, and followed her and Cy into the kitchen. "If you don't mind me asking, what did he have to say?"

She was excited. "A lot. Doug explained everything the company wants to do. He also gave me names of other lease holders in the area. What I don't understand is why Lloyd Montgomery wasn't interested in this idea when he received the letter? Why he didn't at least bring it to my attention?"

"Probably because it wouldn't make money for him," Cy told her. "That man hasn't helped you with anything."

Rachel hadn't been crazy that her father's lawyer had control. "Mr. Montgomery will be gone in a few weeks." She went to the table where the papers were spread out. "I'd like it if you both read over this lease. Your opinions mean a lot to me."

Cy shook his head. "I'll take care of the horses, Cole, you stay and do it." The foreman walked out the door before anyone could argue.

She brushed the braid off her shoulder and looked at Cole. "Would you?"

He nodded. "I'll read it over, but the decision is still yours."

"But you think it's a good idea?"

"It makes sense and the section of land isn't any good for grazing. And the money will provide a steady income for years." He paused, then added, "I think you should have a lawyer go over it."

"I don't want Lloyd Montgomery involved, and I don't know another lawyer."

Rachel didn't want to go into this blind. She trusted Cole. He'd been with her through some rough times the past week, and as much as she tried not to depend on him, she did…and was still asking. "Do you know anyone who could look over this lease?"

Cole hesitated, then nodded. "He's not from around here, but Atlanta."

Was that where Cole came from? "Do you trust him?"

He nodded slowly. "With my life."

"So you wouldn't mind sending him this?"

She watched the mix of emotions play over his face, then they quickly disappeared. She wanted to reach out and comfort this man, knowing that he held everything inside. There was so much pain.

"Atlanta, is that where you're from?" Texas was a long way from his home.

"A long time ago, but there isn't anything left there for me."

She knew what it felt like to be alone. He'd lost his child…ending his marriage. "You could have a life here, Cole."

Before he could answer, Hannah's cry over the monitor interrupted them. "Sounds like the princess is awake, and I need to get the chores done." He went out the door.

Rachel wanted him to stay at the ranch. She'd come to care for Cole…a lot. And even if he felt anything for her, he hadn't pursued it. Since the night he'd kissed her in the hotel he hadn't come near her.

Maybe that was for the best. Yet, she wanted him to stay at the ranch. But so far she hadn't been able to keep him from leaving. Cole Parrish had to make that decision on his own.

# CHAPTER FIVE

IN HIS room at the bunkhouse, Cole took out his cell phone and punched in Luke Calloway's number. His heart pounded in his ears as he listened to each ring.

Finally the familiar voice spoke his name. "Cole."

"Hello, Luke."

"Well, it's about time you let us know you're still alive," his best friend said. "It's been six months."

Cole couldn't help but smile. "It's nice to know that I'm missed."

A long pause. "Like crazy, friend. But I told you that before you left."

Cole had gotten this lecture each time he called his business partner. "I needed to get away…"

There was a long pause. "That doesn't stop me from worrying about you. I thought we were more than business partners."

"We are. It's just that I couldn't go on…"

"I know, Jillian tried to suck the life out of you." A sigh. "She had no right to blame you."

"Yes, she did, Luke. I was never there for her." He

knew his friend had never been a fan of his wife, and never thought the marriage would survive. And it hadn't. In the end, Cole wasn't sure if it was because he hated to fail at anything, or that he truly missed his old life…missed Jillian.

"Okay, so that chapter of your life is closed. Now come home."

"I'm not ready."

"What about the business?"

Ten years ago, they'd started up a small fiber optics company. They'd both worked around the clock to build the operation. Even though the long hours had been a strain on Cole's marriage, he thought since he was securing their future, Jillian should understand. She hadn't, especially when she'd gone into premature labor and he'd been away on business.

Cole closed his eyes against the painful memory of when he'd gotten home to discover a neighbor had taken his wife to the hospital. By the time he'd arrived at her side, their son was gone. Until that moment, Cole had no idea how much his family had meant to him. But it was too late.

"Maybe you should find someone to buy me out," he suggested.

"Jeez, man…that's a big step. Why don't you think on it a while?"

After eighteen months away, Cole still couldn't go back to his old life and career in Atlanta, but did he want to give it all up? "Okay, I'll think about it," he told his partner. "Luke, I called you for another reason. I need legal advice."

"Are you in trouble?"

Cole chuckled. "No, you wouldn't believe the clean life I'm living."

"Sounds boring."

Cole thought about Rachel. "Maybe to you, but I like it. I have a friend who needs someone to read over a contract before she signs it. If I faxed it to you, would you look it over?"

His partner also had a law degree. "Only if you promise to stay in touch…or at least answer my phone calls."

"Deal. If you promise to stop pressuring me to come back."

"Deal."

"Thanks for your help, Luke."

"What are friends for?"

Cole hung up. Luke had been there for him, but his friend couldn't fill the hole inside him when he'd lost his son…and when his marriage fell apart. It had been easier just to walk away… To try to forget that he'd once had the world by the tail, and he let it all slip away.

Suddenly his thoughts turned to the woman and baby up at the house. Everything that he'd once lost was so close…so close that if he reached out he could touch it.

Some nights there was such a deep ache inside him it was worse than a physical pain. A woman like Rachel Hewitt deserved more than a man who couldn't be there for her. No matter how badly he needed her.

Cole tossed the phone back on the dresser. He had to stop thinking about the past. He turned to the doorway to find Josh standing there. "I'm sorry…I didn't…mean to interrupt you," the teenager said as he started to leave.

"It's okay, Josh. Did you need me for something?"

"It's not important."

"You sure?" The kid never wanted to bother anyone, and attempted to do more chores than he should.

"Cy said Rachel's birthday is Friday." He hesitated. "He wants to have a party for her."

Cy had been bugging Cole all last week about it. He wasn't into parties, but he knew the old guy wanted to do this for Rachel. He doubted that she ever had a party in her life. That alone made him want to help with the celebration. "It's more than her birthday. She inherits the Bar H that day."

Josh smiled. "I know. I'll help with anything you need me to do." He held that old battered hat in his hands. "She's been good to me…to let me stay here."

That was Rachel. She was always doing for everyone else. The changes in Josh showed from her nurturing. Not just with food and clothes, but with the gentle touches and encouragement she lavished on the boy.

"Have you talked to Cy about who he's going to invite…to this party?"

"He has a list." The boy pulled out a folded paper and handed it to him. "There are some people from the church, and Reverend Hicks and his wife, Bud and Mary Campbell and their family."

Cole glanced over the list of twenty people. "Has Cy given any thought to who's going to cook for this party?"

Josh shrugged. "I don't know. I know he's getting a cake from town."

Cole thought he could contribute with food from the deli. He told himself it was the least he could do for the party.

It was her birthday, and she decided she deserved the day off. That morning, Rachel had fed and dressed Hannah in a little pink stretch suit.

"Well, aren't you looking just adorable this morning." She tapped the end of Hannah's small nose.

The baby made a cooing sound as she fisted her little hands. "This is a very special day for us. Did you know that? We're going to have the ranch all to ourselves…and I can run it any way I want…without asking for permission about anything. It's going to be wonderful. Yes, it is," she said as she picked up her niece and kissed her cheek. "So let's go down and start this great day."

Downstairs all three of the men at the table were talking about the workday ahead. She had to admit she liked the kitchen crowded with people.

"Good morning, fellas," she said. They all returned her greeting, then went back to their discussion.

Even though they acted as if it were just any other day, Rachel knew that Cy was up to something. She just didn't know what. And whatever it was, it would have to wait until she got back.

"Well, isn't anyone going to say anything?"

"About what?" Cole asked innocently.

"About what day it is."

"July 24. Oh, why does that sound familiar?" Cy teased.

"That's because I was born on this day." She slapped him on the arm as everyone laughed.

"Well, Happy Birthday," Cole said, and she got one of those rare smiles.

"Happy Birthday, Rachel," Cy said as he got up and hugged her. "I thought we could celebrate tonight. Cole, Josh and me are doing supper for you."

She groaned. "My poor kitchen."

"Your kitchen will be just fine," he insisted.

She looked doubtful. "You're right, I'm not going to worry about it. I'm going into town today. I have a meeting with a certain lawyer."

Cy glanced at Cole. "You need someone to go with you?"

She shook her head. "No, I'll handle it just fine."

"Who's watching the baby?" Josh asked.

"Mary Campbell and her daughter are coming by."

"Amy…Amy Campbell?"

Rachel suddenly realized that Amy and Josh were about the same age. "Did you know Amy from school?"

His face reddened with his nod. "I knew who she was, but I don't think she knew me."

She couldn't miss the show of interest.

The teenager had been at the ranch less than two weeks, but the changes had been remarkable. He'd put on some much needed weight. Of course, the two-plus helpings of food he'd consumed at every meal had a lot to do with it. He also worked hard. Beth hadn't been able to locate his father yet, but the social worker had rushed through the paperwork so Josh could stay. Now, Rachel couldn't imagine him not being here.

"Well, maybe you can get to know her today." She looked at Cy. "Could you guys manage lunch on your own?"

"We'll do fine," Cy assured her. He turned her toward the stairs so she could finish getting ready. "All you're supposed to do today is go into town and enjoy yourself. We'll handle things here."

Rachel knew they were up to something, she just wasn't sure what…and she didn't want to know.

After convincing Rachel that she'd raised four kids, Mary Campbell pushed her out the door and on her way to Fort Stockton. Forty minutes later, she arrived in town, but was a little early for her appointment with the lawyer. So she decided to do some much needed shopping for Hannah.

After all, she was going to be signing the lease for the wind turbines and the first payment would be a very hefty amount. Of course she hadn't finalized anything yet. But after today…she had so many more options. And a future.

At ten o'clock Rachel drew several deep breaths, and walked into Lloyd Montgomery's office, remembering the last time she'd come here. It had been right after they'd buried Gib Hewitt. That day she'd felt betrayed by her father and Lloyd Montgomery. But now she was going to regain control of her life. This was the last time she was going to have to deal with old Monty.

She never cared much for "Monty," but her father trusted him with all the ranch business. That hurt her. She was his daughter. She didn't deserve to have to wait to get her legacy.

She walked up to the receptionist's desk. The young woman smiled at her. "May I help you?"

"I'm Rachel Hewitt and I'm here to see Mr. Montgomery."

"One moment." The woman picked up the receiver and announced her.

In just seconds a man of average height with thinning gray hair came through the office door. Monty was about forty-five and showing his prosperity in his growing waistline. He smiled at her.

"Rachel, it's good to see you."

"Hello, Mr. Montgomery."

"Come on, you can call me Monty," he told her as he guided her through the door. She took a seat on the chair in front of his desk.

His smile was still in place. "I can guess why you're here today. First of all, Happy Birthday, Rachel."

"Thank you."

"Why don't you let me take you to lunch at the La Petit Restaurant…" He started to push the button on the intercom when she stopped him.

"No, Monty, I can't. I need to get back to the ranch. I have Hannah waiting for me."

"Hannah?"

"I sent you notification of Sarah's death. What I didn't tell you is that my sister delivered a baby right before she died. Hannah is her daughter…"

"A baby…" He leaned back in his chair. "That's quite a responsibility."

"Yes, Hannah will be my daughter as soon as I adopt her."

"I see."

She doubted he did, but she wanted to keep things on the business at hand. "So I really can't stay long. I only came by to see if all the papers are in order."

"The papers?"

"The transfer of title and my inheritance so I can take control of the Bar H."

Monty stood. "That's what I want to talk to you about, Rachel. The paperwork is going to take some time, but I was wondering why anything has to change. I'm sure your father would be happy if we continue to work together."

*Together*! She didn't like his idea. In fact it angered her. "That's the reason I called you last week, so you wouldn't forget about this day. But you never returned my calls.

"My father's will states that I take control of the Bar H Ranch on my thirtieth birthday. That's today. I want the title and all monies turned over to me."

He stared at her as if trying to intimidate her. "Rachel, you can't run the ranch."

"I disagree, but that's not for you to decide." She stood and glanced at her watch. "Mr. Montgomery, you have until three o'clock today to have the title transferred into my name."

"Rachel, it can't possibly be done that quickly."

"I think it can, and if not, my lawyer will have to contact you. And you aren't going to like the consequences."

Monty glared at her, and she hoped he wouldn't call her bluff. She didn't have a lawyer, just the one that Cole had look over her wind turbines contract.

"Your father wouldn't be happy with your attitude. He had plans for the ranch…plans I can help you with."

"If you ever wanted to help me, you could have done so before now."

He didn't seem to know what to say to that. "I hope you won't be sorry after making this rash decision."

"Believe me, Monty, this isn't a rash decision. I just want what is mine. So I'll see you back here at three o'clock." She turned and walked out, praying he didn't see her shaking. Once outside, she drew a breath and suddenly felt almost giddy.

With each step she felt better, stronger, and she began to enjoy her day along with the view of Main Street. Outside of going to the feed or grocery store, it had been years since she'd come into town just to look around.

There had been a lot of changes to the downtown area with the addition of shops and stores. Maybe with her running the ranch, she'd be able to hire more help and come into town more often.

Gib Hewitt hadn't been a social person, hadn't had many friends. He'd liked the solitude of the ranch and

Rachel hadn't had any choice but to be the same way…until now.

Now she felt free. Smiling, she continued along the sidewalk and was drawn to the hair salon called Classy Cuts. Absently she tugged at her long braid. She'd never had her hair professionally cut and realized her thick hair had become too time-consuming now that she was caring for Hannah.

Why not have a few inches trimmed off? She went to the door and stepped inside. A young woman about her age with shoulder-length blond hair with wispy bangs looked up from her desk. "May I help you?"

"I would like my hair trimmed."

After fifteen minutes of discussion about a practical style, Jennie began to cut. An hour later, Rachel walked out, minus twelve inches of locks that would go to a charity to make wigs. Still, she had plenty left over to have her hair styled in soft curls around her shoulders, highlighted by her newly made-up face. What surprised Rachel were the stares she was getting from people passing by, especially from men. She couldn't help but wonder what Cole would think of her new look. She might be inexperienced, but she saw the longing in his eyes, remembered his fierce kiss.

She also knew Cole Parrish was the kind of man who could hurt her. He didn't seem to want to erase his past, and he definitely didn't want a future…at least anything permanent.

That wasn't going to stop her transformation. She went to another clothing store and purchased a multicolored skirt, teal blouse and a pair of sandals. She even wore them out of the store. After all, it was her birthday and she wanted to look nice.

After carrying her other packages back to the truck, she found a phone and called to check on Hannah. When she told Mary she'd return home soon, her neighbor insisted she take the day for herself, because she and Amy were having fun with Hannah. Reluctantly Rachel agreed and promised to be home by five.

Before Rachel could decide what to do over the next few hours, she heard her name called. She turned to see Doug Wills.

"Oh, Doug, hello."

"Rachel…" His smile brightened as his gaze roamed over her new outfit, then back to her hair. "I like this new look."

"Thank you." She blushed. "I treated myself to a birthday present."

"Then how about I treat you to a birthday lunch?"

She blinked. He was asking her for a date? "Oh, you don't have to do that…"

"I know, but I want to." He raised an eyebrow. "Unless you're already meeting someone."

She shook her head while noticing his soft green eyes and warm smile. "Oh, no. I just have an appointment with my lawyer later this afternoon." She thought about her decision to go with 21$^{st}$ Century. "And I was planning on talking with you, anyway. As you suggested, my lawyer went over your company's contracts for the wind turbines and the lease agreement, and if you're still interested in my land…we need to talk."

"Then lunch it is." His smile brightened as he took her by the arm and guided her down the sidewalk. "Now we have two things to celebrate."

She liked the sound of that. The only thing she wished was that Cole was here with her. Then she remembered that he wasn't going to be around much longer.

So no matter how she looked at it, she was on her own.

At five o'clock several birthday guests were mingling in the living room. And thanks to Mary Campbell's organizational skills, all the food dishes people brought over for the party were lined up on top of the sideboard in the dining room. The birthday cake was hidden in the office.

There just wasn't a birthday girl.

"Are you sure Rachel said she'd be home by five?" Cole asked the teenager, Amy Campbell, as they stood in the kitchen. The pretty girl's brown eyes widened as she rocked the baby in her arms. "Yes. She told Mama she needed to see Mr. Montgomery one more time before she came home."

"I bet he caused her trouble," Cy said. "I knew he would. We should have gone with her."

"No, she wanted to handle things on her own. Just like the wind turbines lease. You have to let her."

Josh rushed into the kitchen. Even he spruced up for the party, with a new shirt and shined boots. But Cole had a feeling it was more to draw the interest of Amy. "She's here. Rachel's truck coming up the road."

"Okay, son, go and let everyone know," Cy instructed him. "And keep them quiet until I bring her in."

Cole knew how much Cy wanted this party to go off as planned. The guests had even parked behind the barn so Rachel wouldn't see their vehicles. He stood back as everyone manned their stations. Mary took the baby, and Amy followed Josh into the living room to find places to hide the people.

To his surprise, he felt his excitement grow as the back door opened and Rachel walked into the kitchen. But to his surprise, it wasn't the same woman who'd left that morning. This one had soft sexy curls around her pretty oval face. Her golden-brown eyes were highlighted by color, but not overdone. Her bright colored blouse showed off her figure as did the skirt that draped over her shapely hips.

"Hi, Cole." She smiled and his heart went soaring into an erratic rhythm.

"Hello, Rachel. Looks like you had quite a day."

"Wonderful!" She gushed as she went to Amy and took Hannah into her arms and hugged her. "Oh, I just missed you to pieces. How was she?"

"A sweetheart." Amy's eyes widened. "Gosh, Rachel, I love your new haircut."

"Thank you, I thought I'd try something different." She glanced around the kitchen. "I thought you guys were going to make supper."

Cole nodded. "We thought we'd eat in the dining room."

Just then Cy came into the kitchen. "Well, look at

you, darlin'." The old man's gaze roamed over her with a big smile.

She blushed. "I thought I needed a change."

"Looks like it's a day of changes." His smile died. "Did you have any trouble with Montgomery?"

"I had some, but we got things ironed out. The Bar H is mine." She waved her hand. "I'll tell you about it later. I'm looking forward to having my birthday supper."

Good for you, Rachel, Cole thought. Recently she seemed to be able to handle a lot of things on her own. That thought left him with an empty feeling in his gut.

Cy grinned. "Okay, let's go." He tugged her hand and led her into the dining room. And the group of people jumped out and yelled, "Surprise."

"Oh, my."

Rachel's heart raced as tears threatened when she saw all the people. They were here for her. For her birthday. Still holding Hannah, she hugged everyone and thanked them for coming.

The reverend gave a blessing and then everyone lined up for food as Rachel took Hannah in the kitchen and prepared her supper. More importantly, she needed the time to herself. She wasn't used to being the center of attention.

She was feeding the baby a bottle when Cole walked in. "I take it you had a hand in this," she said.

He shrugged. "We all helped, but Cy was the mastermind."

She was touched by how many small, subtle things Cole Parrish had done over the past months, but always trying not to be noticed. It hadn't worked. From the day he'd arrived, she'd noticed him.

Mary came into the kitchen as Rachel was burping Hannah. "I'm going to finish this so you can enjoy your party." Reluctantly Rachel gave the baby up and went into the living room and visited with people.

So many of the people came from the church where she attended most Sundays. She'd never done much more than exchange greetings with them. She'd tried to stay involved with the parish by donating things to bake sales or take food when someone passed away. It was the only connection she'd had to anyone outside her father. Gib never allowed people in the house. She glanced around. Things were going to change.

Cy filled glasses with sparkling cider, then he began the toast. "Rachel, you've been like a daughter to this old bachelor. This is a special milestone in your life. Be happy, girl. Today is just the beginning. To Rachel."

"To Rachel," everyone repeated, then drank.

"Open your presents," Josh called out.

She saw that the table in the entry was covered with wrapped packages. "Oh, my. You all didn't have to do this." Emotions clogged her throat. "The party and all of you being here was enough."

"Then I guess we should take them back," Cy called and everyone laughed.

"You don't have to go that far." Rachel took the first gift handed to her and sat down on the sofa. She glanced across the room to see Cole smiling at her and her heart skipped a beat.

Suddenly a knock sounded and someone opened the door. Doug Wills walked in, carrying a bouquet of flowers. "I guess I just got here in time."

"Doug. I'm sorry. I didn't know they were planning a party for me. Everyone this is Doug Wills."

Rachel was happy to see him because he was going to be a vital part of her future. She glanced across the room to see that the man she also wanted in her future was gone.

# CHAPTER SIX

HE COULD hear the singing from the bunkhouse.

Cole smiled despite his misery as he stood at the window and looked up at the house. Rachel deserved this party, and the way her life was changing, it was the first of many.

He was happy for her. She had opportunities now that she hadn't had a few months ago. Most importantly, she wasn't alone anymore. Not like the day he'd showed up to answer her ad for a ranch hand. Besides Cy, she had Hannah…and Josh. Her family. And maybe even…Doug Wills. The man was definitely interested in her.

The thought stirred something inside him. He wanted to think it was just because he was protective of her. Who was he fooling? He was jealous. And he had no right to be. He had nothing to offer a special woman like Rachel Hewitt. And she deserved it all. That didn't mean he had to stand around and watch the man flirt with her.

Hell, he had to get away from here. Next week, he told himself. Next week, he'd leave…for good.

"Cole…"

The sound of Rachel's throaty voice sent shivers through him. He turned around to see her standing in the doorway to his room. The soft light from the hallway glowed behind her head like a halo.

"Rachel…what are you doing here?"

"I came to find you," she said. "Why did you leave the party?"

"I thought it was time." He nodded toward the house. "You should be with your guests."

"Everyone's busy eating cake. I brought you a piece." She held out a plate filled with chocolate cake, then came into the room and placed it on the dresser. That was when he noticed the small wrapped gift she had in her other hand. The one he bought her.

"Are you enjoying your party?"

"Oh, yes. I've never had a party before. Thank you so much, Cole."

"I didn't do anything. It was Cy, and Mary helped organize the food."

Rachel was nervous. When Cole had disappeared from the house, she suspected it was because of Doug's appearance and that gave her fleeting hope that he might care for her. A little.

"It was still nice of you. It was nice that you bought me this gift, too." She gripped the tiny square box.

He hadn't moved. "You haven't even opened it. You might not like it."

"If it came from you, I'll like it. That's the reason I want to open it with you."

Rachel had tried to understand this man, but he held so much back. She guessed the loss of his family kept him from reaching out to people. "Do you mind?"

His gray eyes held hers. "It's your present."

She pulled off the ribbon, then tore through the paper to a velvet box. She lifted the lid to find a silver heart nestled inside. Her fingers shook as she picked up the chain and held it up.

"Oh, Cole, it's beautiful."

"It's a locket."

She set the box down on the dresser and examined the locket closely by the lamp. Finding the clasp, she pressed it and the heart opened into two. She gasped on seeing two pictures inside. One of Hannah and the other of a teenage Sarah. Tears automatically stung her eyes.

"Oh, Cole. How? Where did you get…?"

He shrugged. "We took a picture of Hannah, and Cy found one of Sarah."

"Was that the day he told me he wanted to look for that old rocking chair in the attic?"

He nodded as his mouth twitched, fighting a smile. "It was the only way he could get a picture without you knowing."

"It's a wonderful gift, Cole. So thoughtful. I'll cherish it always."

He stepped closer. "Rachel, I know how much your sister meant to you. This way I thought you could have her close…"

She blinked back more tears, but one escaped and she quickly brushed it away. Why did he have to be so nice? As hard as she tried, she couldn't stop from loving this man.

"I love it. Please, will you put it on for me?" She handed it to him, then turned around and held her hair out of the way.

It seemed she waited for a long time, wondering if he'd refuse, then finally she felt him move closer, his warm breath against her neck, and the brush of his fingers. A warm shiver ran down her spine.

"There, that should do it." He didn't step back, and she didn't, either. The heat of his body seemed to permeate her skin. She ached for his touch…his caress. It was pure agony.

"You didn't tell me if you like my hair."

"Your hair is beautiful no matter how you wear it. But yes, I like it."

Feeling brave, she turned around, clutching the locket in her palm as if it were her safety net.

"Every man at the party was noticing you, too."

She swallowed. "I don't care what every man thinks…just you."

"Rachel, you shouldn't say that." His eyes searched hers as he reached out his hand to touch her face, then pulled back. "You know I'll be leaving."

Her heart lodged in her throat. It had been a few weeks since he'd mentioned moving on, and she'd been hoping he'd changed his mind. "Things are different now, Cole. I can pay you so much more."

"Rachel, you know that's not the reason I'm leaving."

"Is it me?" she asked.

Cole couldn't stand hurting Rachel anymore. He cared too much for her. More than he ever wanted to feel for another woman again. She made him need, made him want.

"No, never you. It's just I need a change."

"The Bar H could be your home."

"I don't want a home any longer." He hesitated. "And that's the way I like it." It was a lie.

"What about needing someone?" She rested her hands against his chest. He felt the burn clear through his shirt.

"I try not to need."

"It's impossible not to need someone. We needed each other that night in San Antonio." Her voice was breathy as large golden eyes looked into his. He hated that she saw so much. "If I had been experienced… would you have made love to me?"

He sucked air into his lungs. "Damn, Rachel. You shouldn't ask a guy that question."

"Why? I just want to know if you wanted me that night."

He blew out a long breath, but it didn't diminish the need or the desire. "Yes, I wanted you. You're a beautiful woman."

She rewarded him with a shy smile. "I have a confession, too. I didn't want you to stop kissing me." Her eyes widened. "And I want you to kiss me now, Cole."

He froze. "This isn't wise."

"Why? Are you afraid of a little kiss? A birthday kiss."

He searched her luminous eyes that were bright with trust…and desire. "Rachel, this is a bad idea."

"No, it's not. I'm not eighteen, Cole. I'm a woman who knows what she wants."

Pure and simple, she was torturing him. He told himself that one little kiss wouldn't hurt…but he knew he didn't want to stop there. Before he could react, she took it out of his hands.

She sighed. "Okay, then I'll kiss you."

Rachel reached up on her toes and leaned into him. He caught the fresh scent of her shampoo just as her lips grazed his and he lost all coherent thought. She eased away and looked at him with that wide-eyed stare, then came back for more. She put her hands around his neck, combing her fingers in his hair while her mouth slanted over his.

A shudder went through him and all resistance disappeared. With a groan, he wrapped his arms around her waist and drew her against him. Night after night, he'd dreamed this. Although it wasn't right, it didn't stop his need for her.

He touched the seam of her lips with his tongue, then slowly delved inside and tasted what he'd been starved for for so long. He was trying to keep it gentle, coaxing her into the pleasure that was killing him piece by piece.

When her hands moved over his chest, he nearly lost it. He made a sound of surrender and pulled her tighter against his body. He let her know what she was doing to him, and this time she whimpered.

Finally he managed to gather strength to end the kiss. But seeing the desire mirrored in her face, he nearly changed his mind about sending her away. He quickly stepped back. "You got your birthday kiss, now go back to the house."

She looked dazed. "Cole…"

He put more space between them. "Come on, Rachel, it was fun, but we both know that it has to end here."

She looked hurt, but he stood tough. He had to. It was the only protection he had against her. "We're too different. I tried the home and family thing. It didn't work." He clenched his hands. "Today is a new beginning for you. You don't need me."

Before she could say a word they were interrupted by voices coming from the porch. "Sounds like your guests are leaving. You need to go."

Rachel started to walk out, then glanced back at him. "I never expected you to take the easy way out," she said then disappeared from the room.

"Believe me, this isn't the easy way," he whispered to an empty room.

Rachel had survived the night, but she hadn't gotten much sleep. Somewhere around three in the morning she'd decided Cole had been right—she didn't need him. It was time she made a life for herself.

She finished feeding Hannah, and placed her in the carrier to start breakfast. Cy and Josh walked in talking about their day ahead.

"Well, good morning, birthday girl."

"Good morning," she returned with a forced smile. "Thanks again for the wonderful party."

"We're so glad you had fun."

"The best ever," she assured him. Cy knew how her father had ignored all birthdays and holidays. "Are you going to be around today?"

"Why, did we forget to clean up?"

"No, the house looks perfect. It's just that Doug Wills is coming by later today. I'm signing the contracts with 21$^{st}$ Century for the wind turbines. I want a little support."

"Well, I'll be doggone." Cy beamed as he hugged her. "Now you can make those improvements around here you've talked about."

Rachel placed a tray of biscuits in the oven, thinking about the large amount of money she would receive for signing the lease. It definitely was going to come in handy.

"I'm not going on a wild spending spree, but the house and barns could use some repairs and paint. A new roof is a must."

Cy sat down as Josh took orange juice from the refrigerator. "You should get a new truck," the teenager said as he smiled down at a cooing Hannah, who was enjoying the attention.

"Maybe a newer one for now." Then the idea came to her that Josh could use the old one. He'd tuned it and fixed a few minor things already. "So I guess I should retire old Betsy, unless there is someone around here who can use it."

Josh looked at Rachel. "You want to sell it?"

"I was thinking about donating it to a friend…like you, maybe."

He blinked. "You want me to have your truck?"

She shrugged. "Betsy needs some new tires and what I pay for chores should be enough to cover your insurance. But when school starts you have to keep your grades up."

"You mean it?"

Rachel glanced at Cy to see his approval. "I mean it."

Josh came to her and hugged her. "Thanks, Rachel. Nobody has ever given me anything so nice."

She hugged him back. "You've earned it, Josh. We couldn't run this place without you."

"Yeah, who'd muck out all the horse stalls?" Cy joked.

Josh smiled at the foreman's teasing, then quickly sobered. "I wouldn't have a place to live if it weren't for you taking me in." His voice was barely a whisper.

In less than a month's time, Rachel had gotten used to him here. Now, Josh had become like a part of the family. Her family. She liked the sound of that. "And you'll always have a home here as long as you like."

"Thanks." He blew out a long breath. "So…when are you going to get your new truck?"

Suddenly the door opened and Cole walked into the kitchen dressed in his usual worn jeans and Western shirt. Rachel's heart began to race.

"Morning." He hung his black hat on the hook and went to the sink to wash his hands.

Josh rushed to him. "Guess what? Rachel's getting a new truck. She's going to let me have her old one."

Rachel realized she was waiting for Cole's reaction. Then he looked at her and smiled. "Is that so?"

"Yeah, I just have to get my own insurance and keep my grades up."

Wiping his hands on the towel, Cole leaned against the counter. "Sounds like a good deal. I'd take it."

"Yeah." The teenager turned to Rachel. "If you want I can do more work around here."

"Josh, no. You do enough as it is." Hannah began to fuss and Rachel went to the carrier to put the pacifier back into her mouth. "You've proven to me that you're mature enough to have a vehicle, but there will be rules…lots of rules. And I need to discuss it with Beth, too."

Josh nodded as if he couldn't say anything, then turned back to the job of breakfast.

In the past month since baby Hannah's arrival, she had to let the men take over some of the breakfast duties. Funny how the three large bodies moved around the space as if it were a practiced routine. A routine she'd like to continue.

Rachel's attention turned to Cole. His rejection last night, it hadn't stopped her from reliving their kiss again and again. The feel of his strength, mixed with his gentle touches, set a yearning in her that she'd never experienced before. She wanted more…

Cole felt Rachel watching him. She was probably figuring several ways to torture him. He didn't blame her. He deserved it, knowing he never should have kissed her in the first place.

He'd thought about skipping breakfast this morning, but knew that would draw questions. All he had to do was act normal and stick to his plan to leave on Monday. Five days to go.

He poured himself coffee and turned around as Rachel tossed her head back and laughed at something Cy said. Her shorter haircut allowed her sleep-mussed curls to dance around her face. He shook his head. He didn't need to think about Rachel in bed.

He went to the table to join the others. "So you're spending your inheritance on a new truck." He sat down across from her.

"My father never had any money to leave me."

"Are you sure Montgomery was truthful about that?"

"Yes. I've known for years the ranch was barely surviving. Of course when Lloyd took over he never once showed any desire to help me change that…not even when a wind turbine company wanted to lease Bar H land."

Old Monty was a jerk. "Are you saying he had plans to swindle you out of this deal?"

She shrugged. "Lloyd would never admit that, but he did want me to agree to continue the trusteeship. When I wouldn't go for it, he offered to buy part of the ranch."

"Let me guess, the Rocky Ridge section."

She smiled and his gut tightened. "Exactly."

"I hope you told him what you thought of him."

"No, but I got the satisfaction of telling him about the lease deal with 21st Century. He couldn't hide his surprise."

"You were lucky you found that letter in the trash."

"No, I was lucky that you had your friend look over the lease. I can't thank you enough, Cole."

Their gazes locked. "You're welcome."

Cy and Josh came to the table carrying bacon and eggs and took their seats. Cole glanced around the table, the shared conversation between the group. He'd gotten used to everyone here, liked everyone here... That was the problem. He was too attached.

Good thing he was moving on.

"Just sign right here," Doug Wills instructed her.

That afternoon in the ranch office, Rachel took the pen from Doug, and after a glance at Cy and Cole, she signed her name along the bottom.

"Initial here and here," he instructed.

Rachel did. "Any more?"

"No, that's it." Doug handed her a copy. "And here's your signing check."

Rachel glanced at the seventy-five thousand dollar amount and her pulse shot off in excitement. It was a lot of money, but it wouldn't be if she wasn't careful with it. That was why she was going to put aside a portion for Hannah's college, and some in the savings, then the rest into the ranch.

"And once the wind turbines are constructed and operational, you'll start receiving royalty checks every month, which will automatically be deposited into your bank account. Is that agreeable to you?"

"It sounds wonderful," Rachel said.

"It's a good deal for us, too," Doug said. "If there

is anything you have questions about, please feel free to call me. Anytime."

"Thank you so much, Doug. I will."

Cole watched as Wills held onto Rachel's hand. It was obvious that he wanted her for more than just business. But Cole wasn't sure if Doug was the right man for Rachel. Besides, she wasn't experienced when it came to men.

The two walked out and Rachel escorted him down the steps. Cole stood at the window and watched as Wills lingered by the car, reaching for her hand. The couple laughed together.

"It's nice that someone is giving Rachel some attention," Cy said as he came up behind Cole.

"Do we know anything about him?"

The older man shrugged. "The reverend said he attends church every Sunday. He worked with the youth baseball program."

Great, Wills sounded like he was a candidate for sainthood. "He's a better man than me."

"Hey, just because a man spends Sunday morning on his knees doesn't mean he's good through the rest of the week. But I don't think it's our opinion that matters. Rachel will decide for herself." The old man grinned. "But I suspect in a short time, she's going to have a lot of men to choose from."

The woman in question finally came back into the office, a big smile on her face. "I know we just celebrated my birthday last night, but we can't let this day go by without doing something. How about we all go into town for dinner?" She waved the check in the air. "My treat."

Rachel's excitement was contagious as later that afternoon, Cole drove them all into town in his truck. After a stop at the bank to deposit the check, Josh convinced them to go to the dealership and just look at some new trucks.

Hannah cooperated while they wandered through the car lot. There were several good deals, and with Rachel paying cash, the deals got even better. She finally decided on a used crew-cab truck that had low mileage and a full-size backseat for Hannah's carrier.

She signed the papers and wrote out a check from her account where the money had been deposited less than an hour ago. The foursome walked down the street to the restaurant.

"I can't believe I bought a truck," Rachel groaned as she set Hannah's carrier in the wide, large booth seat at the steak house. She looked across the table at Cole.

"Buyer's remorse?" he asked.

"Yes! No!" She hedged. "Are you sure it was a good deal?"

"You practically had the salesman on his knees," Cole said. "And he threw in the extended warrantee."

"What else you going to buy?" Josh asked.

"Dinner…and that's all."

"So, it's the biggest steak on the menu," Cy joked as he looked over his choices.

Rachel glanced down to see that Hannah was starting to stir so when the waitress came by to take their order she gave her a bottle to heat.

"Stop frowning, girl," Cy said. "You needed a dependable vehicle. You have a baby now."

"I know. It's just that I've never spent so much money before." She thought about the soft blue color and the nice bucket seats. "Is it practical?"

"It is for you," the older man said. "Since you have the old flatbed truck to cart hay and feed, I'd say it's whatever you want it to be."

She started to answer when she saw a man staring at her. Finally he smiled as he approached the table. "Rachel... Rachel Hewitt?"

"Yes, I'm Rachel," she answered, feeling a flush cover her cheek at the man's close scrutiny. Did she know him? Not that she would forget a tall, handsome blond-haired man.

"Vince Hayden. We went to high school together."

"Oh, my." The Vince Hayden she knew wouldn't give her the time of day. "It's nice to see you, Vince."

"It's nice to see you, too." His gaze roamed over her boldly. "The years have been good to you."

He was flirting with her. "Thank you." She didn't know what else to say to him, so she introduced everyone. "Vince this is Cy Parks, Josh Owens and Cole Parrish." She didn't feel she needed to give any more explanation.

Just then Hannah decided to make her presence known. Rachel unfastened her safety harness, picked her up and tried to soothe her. It wasn't working and she began to cry.

"I'll go see about her bottle." Cole got up and walked away.

Rachel wanted to call him back. She glanced at Cy, who looked amused over the situation.

Vince didn't move. "So…it looks like congratulations are in order. I didn't know you'd gotten married."

She shook her head. "I didn't. Hannah is my niece, but I'm raising her." Why was she explaining her situation?

His smile was back. "I can see that you're busy right now." He glanced around the table, then looked back at her. "Are you still living on the ranch?"

"Yes, I run the place now."

He nodded. "It was nice seeing you again, Rachel. Goodbye," he said, then turned and walked away.

"Wow, Rachel," Josh said. "Vince Hayden… That was Vince Hayden, the quarterback who broke all school records and went to the state championship."

Rachel watched Vince cross the restaurant just as Cole was on his way back to the table. The two men exchanged a nod and a few words. "I remember him from school," she told him. "But the funny thing of it is, he didn't know me. At least he never spoke to me."

The teenager grinned. "Well, he's noticing you now."

Rachel didn't want Vince's attention. She watched as the men parted and Cole started for the table. His long, lazy gait ate up the distance easily. His gaze locked with hers, and a strange feeling erupted in her. She felt her stomach tighten as Cole came toward her.

She only wanted this man.

## CHAPTER SEVEN

"NO, GIVE it a little gas and ease off the clutch," Cole instructed as he looked down at the buried truck wheel spinning in the saturated earth.

"Hold it," he called to Josh. "This isn't working. We need to do something else."

Josh climbed out of the cab and gingerly stepped through the mud as Cole reached for the shovels in the bed. "Start digging."

Both men went to work. "I'm sorry, Cole."

"Hey, it happens. I'm just glad you didn't get hurt."

"I should know better," Josh said. "With the heavy rain last night the field would be flooded."

He scooped up another shovel full of dirt and tossed it away. "Cole, can I ask you a question?"

"Sure. I just can't guarantee that I'll have an answer."

The kid hesitated. "I was just wondering if…can you tell me how to ask a girl out on a date?"

Cole took off his hat and wiped his forehead. He hadn't expected this discussion. "Well, that isn't real easy to answer. I'd say the best approach is just ask her straight out." He leaned against the tailgate. "I take it you're talking about Amy Campbell."

He nodded. "She's so pretty. I can't believe she even talks to me."

From what Cole had seen, Amy was just as interested in Josh as he was in her. "You might be surprised. Usually if the girl spends time with you... she's interested."

"You think so?"

Cole shrugged. "Only one way to find out."

"I still need to get my driver's license. And Rachel might change her mind when she hears about this."

"Why? You had permission to drive around the ranch." He shrugged. "Besides, I was with you. And if you need to, you could just ride over on horseback to see Amy."

Josh looked thoughtful, then went back to shoveling dirt. "You mean just go over to her house? What do I say to her when I get there?"

Cole had forgotten how painful this age was. "You two seemed to be talking just fine at the party."

"That was different. We had Hannah...and the party to talk about."

"Then find other topics. Music, school...you getting to drive soon." He tossed the shovel aside. "Now, let's get this truck out of here."

Josh nodded, climbed in the cab and started the engine.

"Okay, give it a little gas," Cole called out as he leaned his body against the rear fender and began to rock the truck. The wheels started to spin, flinging mud up at him, but he refused to let go until finally the truck gained traction and moved forward out of the hole.

Josh stopped the truck and climbed out. He fought a smile on seeing Cole's mud-splattered clothes. "Oh, Cole, I'm sorry."

Cole wiped mud from his face with a clean spot on his sleeve. "You don't seem real sorry."

"I am." Josh burst out laughing and Cole enjoyed watching the boy let go.

"Well, let's just see how you like being covered with half the pasture." Cole leaned down and scooped up a handful of wet soil.

"No, Cole. I'm sorry I laughed." Josh backed up, then turned and darted around the truck.

"How sorry?" Cole teased, going after him.

"Whatever you want. I'll wash your clothes."

Cole stopped. "Keep talking."

"I'll wash your truck." Something caught Josh's attention and he waved. "It's Rachel."

At first Cole thought it was a trick until he caught the figure on the horse. "What's she doing out here?" Had something happened to Hannah?

Rachel sat tall and straight astride Stormy, her cheeks rosy and hair flying in the wind. She was total grace on horseback.

"So here's where you two have been holed up for the past two hours."

"We had a little problem with the truck," Cole said. "Is something wrong?"

She shook her head. "No, Hannah went down for her nap. Cy is with her." She climbed down and gave him the once-over. "It looks like you had a little trouble, though."

"I was helping Josh get the truck out of the ditch."

She glanced at Josh. "Well, seems you got it done." Her full mouth twitched in amusement and his gut tightened.

He pushed aside the feeling and said, "What brings you out here?"

The wind had picked up and she pushed her straw cowboy hat further down on her head. "When Amy stopped by earlier…"

"Amy was at the house?" Josh asked as he walked toward them.

Rachel nodded. "Yes, I asked her if she'd like to babysit a few hours a day until school begins. So I can get out of the house and help look after things. Anyway, Amy left her cell phone. She called a while ago and asked if…Josh could run it by her house."

The teenager's face reddened. "Me? She asked for me?"

Rachel held out the phone. "Why don't you ride Stormy over and I'll go back in the truck with Cole. Just make sure you're home before dark."

"Really?" Josh looked at Cole.

"I'd say the girl wants to spend time with you," Cole told him. "You better get going."

Josh took the phone and the horse's reins. "I have chores to finish."

"I'll cover for you," Cole volunteered. "But re-member, you have laundry to do."

Josh held up his hand. "I promise." He swung up

in the saddle. "Thanks, Rachel...thanks Cole." He tugged on the reins and kicked the horse into a run.

Rachel sighed, watching Josh ride off. "Why do I feel I've lost him to another woman?"

Cole picked up the shovel and tossed it into the truck bed. "I doubt that. That boy cares about you. You took him in and gave him a home."

Rachel knew she wasn't the only one who'd helped the boy. "I think there's a little hero worship for you, too."

He frowned. "I haven't done anything."

"You talk to him, but more importantly, you listen." She knew Cole didn't want to belong to this mismatched family, but he did. He fit right in.

The wind blew harder. They both glanced up at the sky to see the sun disappear behind dark clouds.

"Looks like a storm is coming. We better get home," he said.

They headed to the truck through the soggy field. Suddenly Rachel lost her balance and gasped as she began to fall. Cole grabbed her around the waist and pulled her against him before she reached the ground.

She looked up at him to see his intense gray eyes. "You okay?"

She nodded, hoping he couldn't hear the pounding of her heart.

He set her upright, but didn't remove his hold. "The ground is pretty treacherous. I don't want you facedown in the mud."

"I don't want that, either." What she wanted was

for him to lean a few inches closer and kiss her. Her hands gripped his arms.

"Rachel, you have to stop looking at me like that," he breathed. "Or we'll both be in trouble."

She wanted a little trouble. She wanted him. She moved her fingers along his large, muscular forearms. He shivered. "What's a little trouble between friends?"

Before he could answer large raindrops started to fall. "We better get out of here." He helped her to the passenger side of the truck and inside.

As Cole rushed around to the other side, he pulled his shirt from his pants and opened the snaps, then pulled it off, leaving his muscular chest partly covered by a tank style undershirt. He laid the clean side down on the seat, and climbed into the truck as the rain really came down.

"I don't want to get mud on the seat. Josh has it looking pretty good."

"No, Josh wouldn't like that," she said as she stared at his broad shoulders. The rise and fall of his chest. A strange yearning came over her, causing a tingling in her breasts. She finally moved her gaze to his face as the heavy rain sheeted against the windshield.

"We better get back before we get stuck but good," he told her.

All she could do was nod, but in reality she wanted to be stuck here with Cole. But he had other ideas…and none of them seemed to include her in his life.

* * *

By eleven, Cole was usually in bed asleep, but tonight he was too keyed-up. He blamed it on the series of thunderstorms that had passed through earlier.

Thankfully Josh and Stormy had made it back home safely, but not long after, another storm drenched the area. Still it wasn't over. There was a tornado watch until midnight.

His thoughts turned to Rachel. Was she frightened? He knew she had a basement to take the baby to if need be. But would she know to go?

Unable to stay put, he headed out to the barn to check on the horses. Outside the night was still…too still. The only sound was the faint rumble of thunder off in the distance. He had a hunch something was brewing. If Texas weather was anything, it was unpredictable, and it could be violent. A sprinkling of rain hit his face and he turned to the house to see the light on in Rachel's bedroom.

After supper, both he and Cy had expressed their concerns about the storms. Rachel had assured them she'd be okay.

He walked inside the barn, closed the door and started down the concrete aisle. He saw right away the animals were as restless as he was. He reached Duke's stall where the horse was at the gate waiting for some attention.

"Hey, buddy." He rubbed the horse's forehead and got a nudge. "You can't sleep, either?"

The animal blew out a breath and Cole smiled. He was going to miss the chestnut stallion. He was a good cow pony. From the first day, Cole had been drawn to the spirited animal and asked Rachel if she minded that he rode him. She blinked at his question, but said yes. It was a few days later that Cy had told him Duke had been Gib's horse.

Cole wondered what Hewitt would think about how his daughter was running things. He never knew the man, but had a feeling old Gib wouldn't like wind turbines on his land. That alone made him smile. Good for you, Rachel.

With her leasing the land, she would have a good living…a good future. She deserved it all. He also thought about how close he'd come to kissing her this afternoon. As badly as he wanted her, he had to resist. She deserved more than he could offer her.

He sighed. Three more days. He'd be gone and the problem would be solved. She'd forget all about him. He just doubted that he'd ever forget Rachel Hewitt.

Suddenly the wind picked up, rattling the doors, causing the rafters to creak. Duke whinnied and the other horses copied him.

"Whoa, boy," he soothed. "It's just the wind."

Cole didn't believe his own words. That was when he heard the noise, when the wind and rain pounded the old structure. The lights flickered and went out, then there was a noise like the sound of a train. He knew exactly what was happening and he had to get to Rachel. He ran out of the barn just as Cy and Josh met him.

Rachel had survived West Texas weather all her life, because she hadn't been foolish. This wasn't just a thunderstorm and she needed to get down to the basement.

All at once a loud noise came from outside. A tornado. She ran into Hannah's room, snatched the baby from the crib and started for the door as the window gave way and a tree branch broke through, spraying glass everywhere.

Rachel cuddled Hannah tight against her body, but she couldn't get out of the path of the tree. She managed to turn away just as the branch came down on her, hitting her and forcing her to the floor. Stunned, Rachel fought to breathe as the air was knocked out of her, but she was grateful to hear Hannah's insistent cries.

Tears filled Rachel's eyes as she kissed the top of her baby's head. "It's going to be okay, Mama's here. I'm not going to let anything happen to you." *Please God, don't let me break this promise to her.*

"Rachel," Cole's voice called to her.

Even though it was pitch-black, her spirits soared. "We're in Hannah's room," she called out.

She saw the flashlight first, then heard his voice. "Rachel, are you hurt? How is Hannah?"

"Well, as you can tell, she's not real happy, but she's okay." Rachel's head, back and arm started to throb. "And I'd feel better if you could get this tree off me."

"I'll see what I can do."

"Please, tell me Cy and Josh are okay."

"They're fine. In fact they're right here."

"Hi, Rachel," Josh said.

"I'm here, too, darlin'," Cy told her.

"Now, let's get you both out of there."

Cole couldn't seem to stop shaking as he made his way into the nursery. When he saw the branch go through the window, he thought the worst had happened to Rachel and Hannah. After breaking off several small branches, he could see that Rachel's lower back and legs were pinned under the large branch, but the baby was untouched and cradled protectively in her arms. He cleared away enough debris to get down on the floor and crawled to her.

Shadows of light helped him reach her and she gripped his hand tightly. "Hi, sweetheart." He wanted nothing more than to take her in his arms.

"Hi," she was breathing hard, trying to fight the pain.

"I'm going to take Hannah out first."

She released the screaming baby and he backed out with the bundle and handed her to Cy.

Then he went back under the branches, wedging himself close enough until he was lying in front of her. He touched her face, hoping to give her comfort. "Rachel, listen, we're going to get you out of here. But you need to help. Josh and I together are going to lift up on the branch, but we need for you to roll to your right side."

"I think I can."

"Good." He lost all common sense and leaned down and kissed her. Just a fleeting kiss, but he needed some contact with her. He scooted back and stood up. "Josh, get on the other side."

The teenager complied and stood across from him.

"Rachel, when I count to three we'll pull up and you roll over."

"Okay," she agreed.

"One, two, three," he called. "Lift."

He and Josh raised the large branch and heard Rachel's groan. "I'm out," she breathed.

They set their burden down, and Cole climbed over the main branch and reached for her. "Can you feel your legs?"

"Yes," she admitted. "And yes, everything hurts."

Cole smiled in the dark as his hands moved over her bare legs, trying not to think of anything else but examining her for broken bones.

Sheets of rain poured through the broken window and he realized she was shivering. "I don't want to move you if you're seriously hurt."

"I'm not, and I'm going to see if Hannah's okay." She worked to sit up. Finally Cole helped her to her feet, then lifted her into his arms and carried her across the hall into her bedroom. He placed her on the large bed.

Rachel reached for the baby and lifted her in her arms. Ignoring the pain, she placed her precious bundle against her shoulder and began to soothe her.

"It's okay, Hannah, Mama is here."

The cries softened as the baby sighed and finally quieted. That's when Rachel let the tears fall.

That was when she felt the added weight of someone sitting on the bed. "It's okay, Rachel," Cole said. "You're both safe."

The tears came harder and he pulled them both

into his arms. Rachel let go. She hated being weak, but decided just this once it was okay.

Two hours later, Cole sat in the crowded emergency waiting room. It had taken a long time to convince Rachel that she needed to be checked out by a doctor. He suspected she had a concussion. She agreed to go, but only because she was concerned about Hannah.

Cole drove her and Hannah while Josh and Cy stayed back at the ranch to rid the baby nursery of one oak tree. The tornado also had managed to take off part of the roof but the rest of the house had fared okay. The other buildings sustained some damage, too, but it was pretty minimal, considering what could have happened.

Cole flashed back to just hours ago when he'd found Rachel and Hannah buried underneath the tree. A shiver ran down his spine, thinking about how badly mother and baby could have been hurt.

He quickly pushed aside the emotions those two invoked in him. That brought up another problem. He'd be a real louse if he left Rachel shorthanded now. With Cy busy supervising the repairs, Josh couldn't be expected to do all the chores. He would have to advertise for help again.

A young, blond-haired nurse came out and motioned for him to come with her. "The doctor wants to speak with you," she told him, then led him back to one of the many cubicles.

Rachel sat on the bed; there was a bandage on her forehead and her arm in a sling. Hannah was asleep in the carrier. "Is everything okay?"

"Yes, I'm fine. Hannah's fine. We just want to go home."

A middle-aged man in a white coat walked in. "Hello, I'm Dr. Harris." He talked as he glanced over the chart. "Miss Hewitt is pretty lucky. She does have a slight concussion and she's pretty bruised around her shoulder and arm. I'd like to keep her here overnight, but she insists that you'll watch over her the next twenty-four hours." He finally looked at him.

Cole glanced at Rachel's pleading look. "Sure... I can."

The doctor nodded, then turned to Rachel. "I want to see you in my office at the end of the week. And remember no lifting with that bruised shoulder."

"I know," Rachel said.

The doctor handed him a prescription for a pain-killer.

"I'll make sure she gets it," Cole said, then took the baby out to the waiting room while the nurse helped Rachel get dressed.

When she arrived he could see the pain and fatigue in her face. "Come on, let's get you home and to bed," he told her.

"What I need more is to get someone to repair the hole in my house."

He guided her through the exit and outside. "Cy will have called someone to come out in the morning. All you have to worry about is getting better."

They stopped at the truck. "I wish I could, but someone has to run things. I need to hire another ranch hand."

Cole lifted Hannah's carrier into the backseat and locked her into the safety seat base. He closed the door, then walked Rachel around to the passenger side.

"I think you can put that off for a while."

"I can't," she insisted. "You're leaving and Josh will be starting school in another few weeks." That stubborn look of hers bore into him. She wouldn't ask for help if her life depended on it. "Cy isn't capable of running things on his own."

He placed his finger to her lips. It was a mistake to touch her. He quickly pulled away. "If you'd be quiet for a minute I can tell you how it'll be done. I'm staying on."

Rachel's golden-brown gaze widened in surprise. "But you want to leave. You said…"

"I know what I said. But I can't leave you when you can barely move."

"I can manage, Cole."

"I have no doubt you can. Even if it kills you. But I'm staying to help you until you get released from the doctor. So unless you can physically kick me off the ranch, you're stuck with me."

She studied him for a long time. "Look, Cole, you don't have to do that. I can afford to hire another hand."

Dear Lord she was stubborn. "I know, but to train someone and get the repairs done is a lot right now, especially when you're laid up."

She stiffened. "I have Amy to help me with Hannah. And I can deal with a new ranch hand."

Did she want to get rid of him that badly? "Why

is it so hard to accept help? Unless you don't want me to stay."

She glanced away, then back at him. "I don't need your charity, Cole. I know how much you want to move on…"

Hell, he'd give anything if he never had to leave. "It would be best for the both of us."

"What if I don't agree?"

He reached out and touched her cheek. It was so soft and smooth. He took his hand away. "We both know there isn't any future in my staying…but you need me right now, Rachel." The problem was he was starting to need her, too. "So let me help."

"Okay, but you're getting a raise in pay."

He opened his mouth, but she spoke instead. "Take it, or it's no deal."

He smiled at her determination. "You drive a hard bargain."

Rachel could hear Cole's voice calling her, but she couldn't open her eyes.

"Come on, sweetheart, wake up."

"Cole…" she whispered as she curled into his warmth.

"That's right, it's me. Open your eyes for me, Rachel."

She groaned, feeling the pain. "I hurt…"

"I know. You'll feel better after you take your pill… And I need to see those big brown eyes."

She blinked and worked to adjust to the soft light from beside her bed. She also felt Cole's arm around her shoulders, as he braced her to sit up. She felt a little dizzy, but she could focus. There was a man in her bed.

She looked up. "Cole…"

He grinned. "You were expecting someone else?"

She rested her head against his chest. It felt so good to have him here with her. "I'll never tell."

"Well, I'm all you got right now. So show me those gorgeous eyes of yours."

She tilted her head up and opened her eyes. She blinked when he shone a tiny light into them.

He turned it off. "How do you feel?"

"Sleepy and sore…all over."

He rested her head back on the pillow and opened the bottle on the table. "Here, this should help." He handed her the pill and some water.

She took her medicine and drank all the water in the glass, then sank back on the pillow…exhausted. She turned and caught Cole as he walked away. "Don't go…" she whispered.

He turned around. "I need to check on Hannah."

The baby. "Oh, Hannah." She pushed aside the sheet to get up. "I need to feed her."

Cole returned and stopped her from getting up. "She's been fed…about an hour ago."

Tears filled her eyes. "I didn't even hear her cry."

"That's because Josh, Cy and I didn't want you to hear her." He sat down on the bed and drew her against him. "You were hurt, Rachel. Let us help you."

She felt weak as a kitten when she tried to look up at him. "I guess I don't have a choice."

He smiled at her.

She loved that smile. Of course she loved the man. Her head was starting to feel better, but things were a little fuzzy. "Thank you, Cole. Thank you so much for taking care of me." She raised up and placed a kiss on his mouth. She pulled back and he was really blurry. "Don't leave me...please."

He lay her back on the pillow. "I won't leave you tonight." Then he surprised her and leaned down and placed a kiss against her mouth.

If this was a dream she didn't want to wake up.

After lying in bed for the past three days, Rachel was close to going crazy. She'd stopped taking her pain pills mainly because they made her so drowsy.

Now, she had to listen to the constant hammering from the workmen. What was getting to her the most was not being able to care for Hannah. But Amy was doing a great job.

The teenager moved into the house to care for the baby full-time during Rachel's recuperation. That made Josh happy. Naturally the boy had found numerous excuses to come to the house during the day. He was also eager to help with supper...and the dishes.

They all did everything for her. Tired of lying in bed, she began plans of decorating Hannah's room. With Amy's help on how to use her laptop, Rachel easily found several baby stores and hundreds of ideas on the Internet. And the contractor gave her a color chart for the paint.

Of course, the nursery wasn't the only room that needed painting. Enthusiasm had Rachel making plans for the entire house, or at least a fresh coat of paint. Something that her father hadn't done in all the years Rachel could remember. Some of the rooms still bore decades-old wallpaper.

Rachel wanted fresh…new. Why not? She was starting her new life. She was still smiling when Amy appeared in the doorway. The girl didn't look good. "I put Hannah down for her nap."

"Amy, what's the matter?" Rachel asked, getting off the bed.

"I don't feel good, Rachel. I called my mom and she said you shouldn't get near me. She thinks I might have caught the flu from my brothers when they came by yesterday." The girl groaned and hurried out of the room.

Thirty minutes later, Mary arrived to take her sick daughter home, saying she would be back to help out, but didn't want to infect another household.

That was when Cy came up to the house. "Josh isn't feeling so good."

"Oh, no. Amy's got the same thing. She went home with her mother."

Cy frowned. "Are you going to be able to handle things here?"

"I think so." Rachel's arm was still in a sling, but feeling much better. "Hannah's napping right now." She went to the refrigerator and took out a bottle of clear soda, then went to the cupboard for crackers. "Take these down to Josh. And make sure he stays in bed. Wait, maybe he should move up to the house so I can look after him."

"I don't think the boy feels like moving anywhere right now. He's weak as a kitten. Besides, we don't need you or Hannah to get this flu."

A few hours later, it wasn't Rachel who got sick, but Cy. He'd gone to his bed.

Rachel was in the kitchen with Hannah when Cole arrived with a duffel bag in hand. "I guess you're stuck with me."

"Stuck with you for what?"

"Looks like I'm the only one left standing to take care of you and Hannah. Where do you want me to sleep?"

## CHAPTER EIGHT

LATER that night, the house was quiet and everyone was settled in their bedrooms for the night…asleep. Cole should have been, too, because he was exhausted. He'd spent most of the evening arguing with Rachel about moving into the house. She insisted he could stay at the bunkhouse.

He wished he was there. Then he wouldn't be lying wide-awake thinking about the beautiful woman in the next bedroom. He even tried to explain away his feelings by rationalizing he'd been without a female's company for a long time, but it didn't help ease the tension in his body. Or the fact that he'd been attracted to her since the first day he'd arrived at the Bar H.

Cole also knew nothing could come of those feelings. He was a drifter and that seemed to be what he did best.

Suddenly there was a soft whimper. He glanced at the baby monitor on the table next to his double bed. Hannah was awake. He got up, pulled on his jeans and went down the hall to the makeshift nursery. The sewing room furniture had been rearranged to allow for the baby bed and changing table.

With the help of the dim light across the room, Cole made his way to the crib to find Hannah's large eyes looking up at him.

His chest tightened. "Well, look who's awake."

Hannah gave a weak cry as her hands and feet moved excitedly.

"I take it you're hungry." He scooped her up and carried her to the changing table, trying to recall Rachel's instructions. Now, he was on his own. How hard could it be?

Cole opened the snaps on the baby's stretchy suit and managed to remove the wet diaper, then slipped a fresh one under her and closed the tapes. After her sleeper was back in place, he picked her up, placed her in the carrier, then took her down to the kitchen.

Rachel had heard Hannah's cry and fought to keep from going to her. Then a short time later, Cole walked past her door. She couldn't stop her curiosity as she got out of bed and put on her robe. It wasn't that she didn't trust Cole's abilities, but what if he needed her to help him? Besides, she'd missed the one-on-one time she spent with Hannah.

Rachel went down the steps and followed the path of soft light that led into the kitchen. She stopped in the dining room when she heard Cole's voice.

"So you miss your mama? Of course you do, but you have to put up with me for a few days. She'll be better soon, but right now, she needs her rest. I'm not so bad…really."

Hannah made several anxious sounds.

"Don't go cryin' on me, angel. I'm all there is right now. Even Uncle Cy is laid up. And Josh, too. I know it feels like everyone has deserted you, but I promise they'll all be back…real soon."

The baby began to coo.

"That's better. Now, how about the bottle I promised you? I think it's about ready."

Trying to stay hidden, Rachel peered into the doorway and with the help of the light from the stove, she watched as a shirtless Cole took a seat at the table. Tears formed in her eyes seeing the big man cradling tiny Hannah against his muscular chest. Lucky girl.

"Hey, look at you go," he said softly as he stared down at the child. "It's no wonder. When are they going to put you on something you can sink your teeth into? Oh, that's right, you don't have any teeth." He smiled and Rachel's heart tightened. "I bet a little cereal would taste pretty good to you right now."

Hannah released the nipple and made some indistinguishable noises.

"My thoughts exactly." As if Cole sensed her presence, he looked toward the door. "Rachel…I didn't hear you."

She walked in. "I'd say you were pretty busy." She touched her baby's head.

"Did we wake you?"

"No, I guess I've gotten used to getting up about

this time." She loved the fact Hannah's eyes followed her voice. "Would you mind if I stay?"

"Of course not. Why would I?"

She pulled up the chair and caught a whiff of his soap mixed with this man's own scent. She kissed the top of her daughter's head, then raised up to stare right into Cole's silver gaze. "You seem to want to hide this side of yourself."

He didn't break eye contact. "There is no 'this' side of me. But I have to admit we all act a little silly when we're talking to kids."

She hesitated, feeling his breath against her face. "Well, you're very good at it. You have Hannah responding to you."

"She's quite the charmer."

Rachel knew how hard this was for him. "I appreciate you caring for Hannah. I know this can't be easy for you."

Before he diverted his gaze, she could see the flash of emotions. "I can handle it."

"Still it has to bring back memories."

Cole nodded, wanting to ignore her, but Rachel wasn't going away. And selfishly, he didn't want her to. He needed her here, ached to feel her close, to smell her intoxicating scent. Yet, Rachel was a constant reminder of what he couldn't have, but that didn't stop the hunger he had for her. That was what frightened him the most.

He placed Hannah against his shoulder to burp her. "I doubt I'll ever forget." He'd wanted a family of his own for so long. But he'd messed up any chance of that.

"I'm sorry, Cole."

He nodded. "It was a long time ago."

He'd held his feelings in check so far, but if Rachel kept pushing… Then she touched him on the arm. Her tenderness was almost more than he could bear. He worked hard to concentrate on Hannah, but he couldn't. Not with Rachel this close.

"Not so long you've forgotten," she whispered as she leaned toward him.

"Some things never leave you," he said.

Cole's need for Rachel grew until he couldn't deny it. He dipped his head the last few inches and captured her luscious mouth. She sighed and he increased the pressure. He slipped his tongue along her lips, stroking, eager to taste her. He felt her fingers dig into his forearm as their hunger intensified, but holding the baby kept him from going any further. Although it was killing him, it was a good thing. Finally he pulled back as they both worked to slow their breathing.

"Oh, Rachel… No matter how tempting you are this isn't wise."

She looked hurt, but didn't speak.

"Don't make me out to be something I'm not. Sooner or later, I'll let you down." Cradling the half-asleep Hannah, he stood, placed her in the carrier and grabbed the handle. "I better get her to bed." He started out of the kitchen, praying Rachel wouldn't call him back. At the same time, he was wishing he could take comfort in her arms. Make him forget all the pain…and memories of his past.

\* \* \*

"I'm sorry I wasn't here, Rachel," Doug Wills said the next morning. He stared up toward the half-dozen repairmen replacing roof tiles on the house. "I had no idea this happened to you until I got back into town last night."

"It's okay. I'm just grateful the storm only damaged the house."

He stared at her sling. "But you were hurt."

"I'm only a little bruised, Doug. I'm just grateful Hannah is safe. The doctor said I'll be good as new in a few days." She gave him a bright smile.

Rachel never expected to find Doug Wills on her doorstep at 8:00 a.m. Maybe it was a good thing, since Cole hadn't been too talkative as he continued to care for Hannah.

"As you can see, the repairs are nearly finished. I needed a new roof anyway. Among other repairs."

"How are you managing with the baby?"

"I have help. Amy and Cole."

"If there's anything I can do…"

She raised her hand to stop him. "I appreciate your offer, Doug, but I'm fine, really. Besides, isn't this is a little beyond your duties?"

The good-looking salesman smiled. "I'm not doing this out of duty. I care about you, Rachel."

Why couldn't she feel the same way about this man? A good-looking, stable man who had shown interest in her from the beginning. He would probably make a good husband and father. Too bad she wasn't interested, and she needed to tell him.

"Doug. You've been good to me, helping with the

contracts for the wind turbines, but with Hannah so small, my life has to center around her. I'm not ready to start a relationship…with anyone."

Doug looked at her for a long time. "I can't deny that I'm disappointed." He sighed. "I guess I knew from the beginning that you cared about someone else."

"There isn't anyone else."

He cocked an eyebrow. "I'm not blind. I can see there is something between you and Parrish. Whenever the two of you are together sparks fly."

Rachel was shocked at the man's observation. "But Cole doesn't feel the same way. He's been planning to leave for the last month."

Doug shrugged. "Doesn't look like he's so anxious to me…since he's still here."

"Your mother has company, so it's just you and me," Cole said as he lifted a naked Hannah into the plastic tub next to the sink.

Not that he didn't enjoy being with this lovely lady, he just hated the fact he cared that Rachel was spending time with another man.

*Stop. You don't have the right to choose who she sees. Just let her go. She deserves so much more than what you can offer her.* He just wished his brave words could stop his feelings for her.

Propping up the baby with one hand, he took the small washcloth in his other hand as he began the task of soaping her. He saw Hannah's trusting eyes stare up at him and smiled. She looked so much like Rachel. Same dimpled chin, and big round eyes.

After washing the crown of wispy curls on the baby's head without drowning her, he reached for the towel, then wrapped Hannah up securely and carried her to the kitchen table where there was a blanket spread out.

"Hey, we did it," he told her as he laid her on the makeshift changing table. He rubbed her down with lotion and put on the diaper. "Now, it's time for the clothes." He picked up a one-piece, pink sunsuit and was darn proud of himself when he got it on her without too much trouble.

When Rachel walked in, he had Hannah back in the carrier. "Oh, I missed her bath."

"We just finished." He stood back, feeling satisfied. "Want to check behind her ears?"

She smiled at the baby. "No, I trust you."

Rachel had been hoping she'd see a little flicker of awareness from this man. It amazed her how Cole could act as if nothing had happened between them, that they'd never shared a hot kiss in this very kitchen just a dozen hours ago.

Well, she could play the game, too. "Doug stopped by."

His smiled faded. "Is there a problem with the lease?"

Rachel shook her head. "He was just concerned about me." She then leaned down to inhale that wonderful fresh baby smell. "And he wanted to ask me out." She shifted her gaze to Cole, but he didn't say anything. Disappointed, she said, "Maybe you should put her down for her nap."

Cole nodded and followed Rachel upstairs. Luckily Hannah's temporary room was at the far end of the house away from the noise of the repair work.

Rachel smoothed the crib sheet as Cole brought her daughter in and laid her down. He moved into the hallway while she stayed and hummed a lullaby as the child's eyes drooped shut. Silently she backed out of the room and nearly into Cole.

"She asleep?" he asked, looking over her into the room.

She nodded, staring at the man with the front of his shirt soaked, the sleeves rolled up and a baby towel tossed over his broad shoulder. He'd never looked sexier. She pulled the terry cloth away. "Maybe you should go dry off."

He looked down at his shirt. "Your daughter does like to play."

Rachel felt a pull in her chest. "She is my daughter, isn't she?"

"Yes. From the day you brought her home from the hospital."

Rachel rubbed her injured arm. "I just wish I was able to care for her."

"You will," he told her. "When the doctor releases you in a few days."

She nodded. "I'm not used to sitting around doing nothing."

He folded his arms over his chest. "You deserve this time. Since I've been here, I've watched you do too much. And if anyone wanted to help out, you got angry."

She shrugged. "So I'm used to working hard."

"But now, you don't have to. You can hire whoever you want."

"It seems that good men are scarce. I can't seem to find one."

That was a lie, she had found the man she wanted. She just couldn't keep him.

After changing his shirt, Cole came downstairs and told Rachel he was going to check the herd, but promised to be back before Hannah woke up from her nap.

Rachel was restless, too. So she went upstairs and stripped all the beds. She tied up the laundry in a sheet, and with her one good arm, dragged it downstairs. Once the wash cycle began, she did a little cleanup, and reheated some of Mary's homemade soup she'd sent over before everyone took sick.

After another load of laundry, and a quick check on the baby, Rachel managed the handle on the soup pot and went to the bunkhouse to check in on Josh and Cy. She went to the small kitchen area and filled two bowls from the cupboard and headed for Cy's room.

The old foreman was lying down, still looking pale. "How are you feeling?"

He glanced her way. "Rachel, you shouldn't be here."

"Someone has to take care of you."

"I can take care of myself." His weakness showed as he tried to sit up.

Rachel propped another pillow behind his head. "I know you can, but I like to help. How do you feel about a little chicken soup?"

He smiled. "If it's made by you, I'd love some."

She brought in a bowl and set it on the table next to the bed. She then went into Josh's room.

He had on the old television, watching a baseball game. "Looks like you're feeling better today."

Josh grinned. His coloring was much better. "Hi, Rachel. I feel pretty good today. I'm hungry, too."

"Well, that's a good sign. I brought you some soup."

He sat up. "Great." He took the bowl from her and began to eat. "If you want, I can help Cole do the afternoon chores."

"I think you should stay in bed until tomorrow. Cole can handle things."

He frowned. "I was kind of hoping I could call Amy. She was feeling pretty bad yesterday."

"How about I call her mother to find out?"

He couldn't hide his disappointment. "Okay. But will you tell her that I hope she feels better?"

Rachel agreed and gathered up their dirty clothes and returned to the house to start another load of wash. After four days in bed, it felt good to get back to work.

By the time Cole walked in the door, she had a roast in the iron pot on the stove, and she was fixing Hannah a bottle.

"Sorry it took so long," he said as he hung his hat on the peg. "One of the calves got tangled up in the fence." He walked to the sink.

"Is it okay?" She knew how important each calf was for the ranch.

He used the soap to wash up. "Yeah. I had some antibiotic cream in the truck. I'll check on him again in a few days."

Just then a familiar sound came from the monitor. "Sounds like the princess is awake." He left and a few minutes later returned with Hannah.

"Do you think I could feed her?" Rachel asked. "I'll hold her with my good arm."

"Okay, but why don't you sit on the sofa."

Carrying the bottle, she walked into the living room and sat down.

Seeing her excitement, Cole didn't mind giving up his duty. He placed the baby in Rachel's arm and she immediately wrapped a supporting arm under Hannah, trapping his hand against her breast. Her soft, full breast. He tugged it away, but not before he grazed her nipple.

"Sorry," he said, but unable to miss the effect his touch had on her with the hardened nub against her cotton top. Instantly his body stirred and he sank into the chair across from her. He had to think of something else…fast.

"Do Cy and Josh feel well enough to eat?"

"I took them some soup about an hour ago. Josh is already feeling better. So much so he wants to go see Amy."

"How is Amy feeling?"

"I called Mary. She feels a lot better and is anxious to come back tomorrow." She sent him a questioning look. "Do you mind staying another night or so?"

Yes, he minded. She was too close. They slept just a room apart, even shared the same bathroom. It was killing him. "No, I don't."

The phone rang and Cole went to answer it in the kitchen. "Hello."

"Hello, it's Doug Wills, is Rachel there?"

Cole's mood suddenly soured. "Just a minute, I'll get her."

He went into the living room and reached for Hannah. "It's Doug Wills."

"Doug? What could he want?"

"Haven't a clue," he said and she let him take the baby. Cole put the baby against his shoulder as she walked into the kitchen.

A few minutes later he heard her laughter. Big deal. So what if she liked the man. Wills seemed like a decent guy.

Rachel returned. "Seems Doug forgot to go over the starting dates for the work to begin."

"Can't he just mail them to you?"

She shrugged. "He said he wants to go over them with me personally."

"I bet," he murmured.

"What?" she asked.

"Nothing. Just thinking out loud."

"Oh. Well, anyway, I invited him to stay for supper. I just figured he was coming all this way. I mean, he's been so nice about everything."

Yeah, helpful. After getting a burp from the baby,

Cole placed her back in the carrier and moved the handle so her favorite toy dangled in front of her.

"I'd say the man has other ideas, and it has nothing to do with business." He turned and headed out through the kitchen, knowing he was acting foolish. But thanks to Rachel, he was doing all sorts of things that were out of character.

Later in the afternoon, with Hannah back to sleep, Rachel had managed to finish the laundry. She replaced the sheets on her bed, then went into Cole's room.

She should have changed the bed before he came to stay, but she hadn't the chance. It took a little longer with only one good arm, but she kept going until she had the lightweight blanket tucked in. She went back downstairs and brought up the stack of clean boxers, socks and T-shirts.

She knew he would be upset that she'd done his wash, but he'd been doing everyone's job the past two days. Besides, she suspected it had been a long time since anyone took care of Cole. Bundle in hand, she placed his clothes on top of the dresser. That's where she saw his cell phone and numerous coins scattered around, but something else stood out. At first it looked like another coin, then she picked it up. It was a tiny oval-shaped medal with the image of an angel looking down on a baby. She turned it over to read, God Bless Our Baby.

*Cole's son's?*

A heaviness filled her chest as she thought about the pain Cole must be feeling every time he looked at this. Why? Sensing she wasn't alone, she looked up to see Cole in the doorway.

"Oh, Cole. I was just putting away some laundry." She set the medal back down. "And I saw this."

He still didn't say anything.

"Was it for your son?"

With a nod, he walked into the room and picked up the medal. "It was to go in my son's crib." His voice softened. "I know it's silly I still have it." He looked down at the object in his hand. "I'm not even Catholic. But a special person gave it to me."

"Your wife?" Rachel asked. She hated feeling jealous. Was he still in love with her?

He pursed his lips. "No. Jillian didn't want anything in the nursery that wasn't designer. Loretta Simmons gave it to me." His gaze met Rachel's. "Miss Loretta took in foster kids at her ranch. I lived there during my teens. That's where I learned to ride."

Cole had no family. "How long were you in foster care?"

"Since I was ten."

"What about your parents?"

He shrugged. "Mom wasn't quite sure who my daddy was, and when I was about ten, protective services took me away because she couldn't take care of me." His eyes bore into hers. "She was a drug addict."

"Oh, Cole."

He stiffened. "Don't pity me, Rachel. I got over my childhood years ago."

"You never get over losing your parents." She knew what it's like to have her family leave. She brushed a tear away, wishing it still didn't bother her. "It's not pity, Cole, but I do understand."

He didn't say anything for a while. "It was going to be different with my son. I was going to be there for him, I really was… I just didn't get my priorities straight until it was too late."

"I don't believe that."

"It's true," he said. "I was driven to make a success. I worked so much I was never home. And then Jillian went into labor…early."

She could see the pain etched on his face. He blamed himself.

"Did you cause the premature labor?"

He shook his head. "The doctor said there was no reason Jillian's water broke early. Then there were complications with the baby's underdeveloped lungs. He didn't survive."

Rachel reached for him and slipped her arms around his waist. "I'm sorry, Cole." She just held on to him, wanting to absorb some of his hurt. "But it's not your fault. Things like that happen. You've got to forgive yourself, Cole. Let me help you."

"I'm fine…" he told her. "It was a long time ago."

Not long enough that he could close that door.

"It's okay to let me in. I just want to be there for you." She raised up and placed a soft kiss on his mouth.

He sucked in a breath. "Rachel, it's not easy for me to let people in…"

She studied the sadness in his eyes. "I'm here, Cole."

He started to reach for her when the sound of the doorbell broke the spell between them.

Cole stiffened and stepped back. "Your dinner guest is here."

Once again he shut himself away, but she wasn't giving up. This man meant too much to her.

# CHAPTER NINE

RIGHT after they'd finished supper, Cole excused himself and took a bottle upstairs to feed Hannah. He never returned. He told himself he didn't want to disturb Rachel and her dinner guest.

He stood at the window in his bedroom and looked out at the moonlit pasture. Usually the scene helped relax him. Not true this time, with hearing every ripple of laughter that drifted up to the second floor. Then there were the long periods of silence when his mind conjured up all sorts of scenarios.

Most of all, he hated that Rachel was with another man. Although he had no right at all to feel possessive, he did.

He had to stifle his attitude and fast because Hannah was waking up hungry. Unable to wait any longer, he headed downstairs just as the front door closed, and soon after Wills's truck started up.

Cole walked through the house to find Rachel in the kitchen. She had on that T-shirt and colorful skirt that showed off her shapely calves and dainty bare feet. He ignored his racing pulse and noticed her discarded sling on the counter. She was reaching into the high cupboard to put away dishes.

"Just what are you doing?" he called to her.

Rachel jumped as the plates slid from her hand and went crashing to the floor. "Cole, you scared me."

He rushed to her side. "Don't move," he ordered her.

He lifted her up onto the counter. "Stay there. I'm getting the broom."

Rachel was angry—not over the broken dishes, but that she let this man get to her. Even more angry herself that she'd thought Doug would make Cole jealous. The sad thing was she couldn't make him have feelings for her.

Cole returned and began picking up the large pieces from the floor. She pulled her knees up and covered them with her long skirt. "If you get my shoes, I'll help you."

"I caused the mess, I'll clean it up." He swept up the broken pieces and dumped them in the trash.

When she heard Hannah's cries, Rachel refused to sit there. "Stop being stubborn, Cole, and get my shoes. They're by the back door."

"Fine." He retrieved the sandals and handed them to her along with the broom. "Here, you finish up." He went to the refrigerator, took out a bottle and placed it in the bottle warmer.

After putting on her shoes, Rachel slid off the counter and took over the sweeping, trying to understand why Cole was so angry with her. "Did I do something to upset you?"

"You aren't supposed to be using your arm."

"And I haven't been…until today. It feels fine, really."

"Glad to hear it." He took the warmed bottle and walked out.

She followed him up the stairs to her daughter's room. Hannah was fussing as she stepped to the crib. "Hi, sweetie."

The child calmed down a little, but wasn't going to stop until she got fed. Cole lifted her out of the bed and carried her to the changing table. Then he stepped back so Rachel could handle the job.

Rachel didn't hesitate as she changed her daughter's diaper, then tentatively lifted her into her arms. She was still sore, but she couldn't let Cole know. She took the bottle, sat in the rocking chair and began to feed the baby.

She looked up and found Cole had left. Rachel's heart tightened. No matter how close they'd gotten in the past week, he'd pulled away from her again.

She tried to concentrate on Hannah, who did seem happy to have her mother with her. After the baby finished her bottle and burped, Rachel carried her to the crib and laid her down. Hannah's eyes opened, then slowly drifted closed.

"Go to sleep, sweetie." After covering her with a light blanket, Rachel backed out of the room and closed the door.

Now, she had a man to talk to and she wasn't going to let him deny his feelings for her any longer.

\* \* \*

Rachel went down the hall to the guest room. With a quick knock—and before she lost her nerve—she swung open the door to the dimly lit room.

"Cole, we need…to talk—" She stuttered on her words, seeing that he wasn't as prepared to see her. His dark hair was brushed back and still wet from the shower. And he was wearing a towel around his trim waist. And nothing else. "I'm sorry… I should have waited…"

Cole didn't say anything about her intrusion, and she couldn't seem to move. Rachel finally broke the silence. "I want to know why you are so angry with me."

"No, you don't," he told her. "Just leave, Rachel, before I forget…" He paused.

Suddenly she felt brave. It was time she took a chance on something she wanted. "Forget what, Cole? Forget it bothered you that Doug came to see me?"

His intense gaze darted away. "Who you entertain is of no concern to me."

Trembling, she walked toward him. "Yes, it is. And it thrills me that you were jealous."

He shook his head. "I wasn't. Dammit, Rachel. Just get out of here before…"

"Before what? Before you admit you have feelings for me?" She reached out her hand and touched his bare chest. She loved the sensation of the crisp hair against her fingertips, the warmth of his skin. Her gaze traced the width of his shoulders, down his muscular arms, then she did a return journey until she reached his face to see the desire in his eyes.

Her pulse leaped. "I'm not afraid of what's going

on between us, Cole," she breathed. "I've never felt this way before. I've been around cowboys all my life, but not one of them has ever made my heart race, my body ache from wanting…"

His own heart pounded under her fingers. "You shouldn't say that, Rachel." He shut his eyes momentarily. "I'm trying to be the good guy…"

"Stop trying so hard, Cole." She took a step closer to him. "Just let it happen. Just let me know how you feel."

He made a growling sound, and wrapped his arms around her. His mouth covered hers so fast, Rachel didn't have time to take a breath. And yet, she didn't need oxygen as much as she needed this man.

She slid her hands around his neck and leaned into his body. His strong, solid strength that let her know that he desired her.

He tore his mouth away, and scattered tiny kisses along her jaw to her ear. "It drove me crazy thinking about you with Wills. I wanted to beat him to a pulp. Does that make you happy?"

She pulled back and smiled. "It's a start. Keep going."

He wasn't smiling. "I want you, Rachel. There was never any doubt about that. But there isn't any happily ever after for me. I can't offer you what Wills can."

She grew serious. "I don't want Doug. I want you, Cole."

His jaw tightened.

"And I'm not asking for anything other than being

with you right now." She raised up on her toes and kissed him. She used her tongue to trace the seam on his lips and their breath mingled as he opened for her. With a groan, he swiftly took control and deepened the kiss until they were both breathing hard.

Cole was dying a slow death. He wanted to do the right thing and that would be to send Rachel away. But he wasn't that strong, and he was selfish enough to want one night with her. To feel what it would be to love again.

"Just be sure, Rachel."

"I am." Her gaze raked over him. "And it seems I have a lot more clothes on than you." She smiled. "What are you going to do about it?"

Air trapped in his lungs as she tossed out the challenge. He took it and reached for the hem of her T-shirt. "Then lets see what we can do to get you caught up." He pulled the shirt off over her head then tossed it causally aside, leaving her in an ivory lace bra. Every breath she took had her nearly spilling out. He offered up a prayer that he could hold it together…so he could go slow.

"When I bought this that day in town," she began. "I was thinking about you."

"It's beautiful. You're beautiful." He kissed her along the scalloped edge and her breathing grew more labored.

"Let's see if it's a matched set." His hands moved to her skirt, found the zipper, then let it drop to her feet. The high-cut panties did match the bra, and showed off her mile-long legs.

His gaze returned to her face. "Please, Rachel, tell me you're sure about this. I don't think I could stand it if you changed your mind."

She reached for the front clasp on her bra and opened it, allowing it to slide off. "Make love to me, Cole."

"I plan to." He lifted her in his arms and carried her to the bed where he'd already pulled back the covers revealing fresh sheets. "To every inch of you." He leaned over her and took one perfect rosy nipple into his mouth.

She whimpered and cupped his head, holding him to her. He moved to the other breast, eagerly repeating the action. This time she arched her body off the bed, and he knew that all he wanted to do was spend the night pleasuring her.

"Cole…"

"I'm right here. And I'm not leaving you tonight," he promised.

Her dark gaze studied him. "Good, then let's not waste a minute of it." She tugged the towel from his waist and tossed it aside.

Cole pressed his body against hers and began to fulfill his promise…

Just before dawn, Cole lay in bed watching Rachel sleep. Tucked against him, her body aligned perfectly with his. So perfectly that he didn't want to move…didn't want to leave the bed, to break the spell…

To end their incredible night together.

He'd never known anyone as loving…as responsive…and so eager to please him. And her trust in him was humbling. How could he leave her?

Rachel sighed in her sleep, and snuggled closer. He kissed the top of her hair and inhaled her scent. Her hand moved over his stomach and she arched toward him as if seeking pleasure, pleasure he had eagerly shared with her…for most of the night.

First in his bed, then after feeding Hannah, their own hunger took over and they'd ended up in Rachel's bed eager for each other again. Now as the sun threatened to bring the new day, their time together was nearly over. He'd been foolish enough to think one night would satisfy his hunger for Rachel.

A lifetime would never be enough.

He frowned. He couldn't offer her a lifetime. He'd end up letting her down. He couldn't do that to Rachel…not when he cared so much.

Rachel murmured his name as her body arched against his while her hands moved over him. It killed him, but he stopped her advances, knowing he had to deny them both what they wanted.

"Cole…" she breathed.

"Go back to sleep, Rachel," he whispered. He leaned over her and placed a kiss on her tempting mouth. "Hannah's awake," he lied. "I'll go check on her."

Before he could change his mind, Cole slid out of bed. For a moment, he stood and watched her in the dim light as she snuggled back into the pillow and closed her eyes.

He retrieved his jeans from the floor and slipped them on, then went down the hall to the baby's room.

In the last few days, he'd gotten used to the time he'd spent with Hannah. At first it had been hard, reminding him of what he'd never have with his own child. But the sadness slowly faded as he'd gotten to know and love this little girl.

*Yeah, you lost your heart to her big time.* His thoughts turned to the woman asleep in the other room. The same thing had happened with the mother.

He went to the window and looked out toward the big faded red barn and corral. Not far away was the bunkhouse and the foreman's cottage along with several outbuildings. They all needed repairs and paint.

No doubt, years ago the Bar H had been a showcase. And now that Rachel had the financial means, it would probably be again. His chest grew tight, and he'd wished he could be here to help bring the place back, maybe talk to her about breeding some good saddle horses...

But he couldn't stay.

It was time to go. This time he'd be leaving more than he ever dreamed. His heart.

The warm sunlight woke her. Rachel sat up in bed and glanced at the clock. It was nearly 8:00 a.m. She'd overslept.

A flashback brought memories from her night with Cole. She felt a heated blush rise to her face, recalling what a generous lover Cole had been.

She glanced toward the empty side of the bed. She didn't expect him to be there. It was after dawn and someone had to care for Hannah and handle chores.

She slipped out of bed. Naked, she reached for her robe and went into Hannah's room to find her gone. She wanted to go downstairs and be with both Hannah and Cole, but what if Cy and Josh were in the kitchen, too? How would she explain why she wasn't dressed? She headed for the bathroom.

After a quick shower, she put on her regular work clothes of jeans, shirt and boots. Thirty minutes later, she went down to the kitchen looking forward to seeing Cole. Instead she found Amy with Hannah.

Rachel put on a smile. "Good morning, Amy."

"Oh, hi, Rachel."

"You sure look a lot better than the other day. How do you feel?"

"Much better," the teenager said as she placed the baby in the carrier. "I'm sorry I left you alone with Hannah."

"It couldn't be helped." Rachel raised her once-injured arm. "Besides, I feel fine. But I'd like to have you babysit for a few hours a day until school starts."

"I'd like that."

Josh rushed in the back door. "I got the eggs from the henhouse," he said as he sat the basket down. "Oh, Rachel, you're awake. Good, we can eat."

"Sorry, I guess I held things up."

"Cole told us to let you sleep since you were up with Hannah." He grinned at the happy baby in the carrier. "Amy and I already started breakfast. Just waiting on the eggs."

Cole. Where was he? She wished that she could have seen him first…and alone. "Where is Cole?"

"He rode out earlier to check the herd. He said not to hold breakfast for him."

As the two teenagers moved around the kitchen, Rachel sank into her chair at the table trying not to look disappointed. She couldn't help but think he was avoiding her. She guessed she should be grateful that there wasn't any awkward morning-after scene.

Cole walked up the porch steps. He couldn't put off seeing Rachel any longer. Being with her last night had affected him in ways he wasn't ready to face. So much so he needed to get away for a while, so when Amy had arrived this morning he turned Hannah over to her. He'd gone to the barn, saddled Duke and went off for a ride.

It hadn't helped. Rachel was still there. In his head…seeped into his body…into his heart. And it had been a mistake to fall into temptation. It couldn't change anything. He still had to leave.

He heard a sudden burst of laughter from the kitchen. The sounds of a family. Rachel's family. Not his. Never his. His chest tightened and he paused to get it together. He put on a smile and pulled open the door. They were all seated around the table eating breakfast.

"Morning," he called out.

"Morning," came back in unison.

"How's the herd?" Cy asked. "Any problems?"

"None." He started for the stove and caught Rachel's gaze. She gave him a shy smile and he nodded back as if it were any other day. Ignoring the fact that they'd shared a bed and their bodies. His hand shook as he scooped up eggs and a few pieces of bacon. He walked to the table and sat down.

"What do you want me to do today?" Josh asked.

Cole swallowed his forkful of eggs. "Maybe you should ask Rachel. Seems she's well enough now to handle things."

"I do feel better," she said and he didn't miss her hurt look. She turned to Josh. "How about you go into town for groceries?"

"You want me to drive into town?"

"Well, you have your license now."

"I guess I do." Josh's excitement died when he looked at Amy.

"Amy, why don't you go with him," Rachel suggested. "That way you can get the shopping done faster, and you have a cell phone in case something happens."

"What about Hannah?" the girl asked.

"She's going down for her nap soon. Besides, I've missed spending time with her."

Josh got the list from Rachel, then Cy caught him. "We could use some things from the feed store, too." The foreman walked out with the couple, leaving Rachel and Cole alone.

Before Cole could say anything, Rachel went to Hannah and lifted the carrier off the counter.

"I can get that for you," Cole said as he stood.

"No, I can do it." She walked out of the room.

Okay, he handled this morning all wrong. Somehow, he had to try to fix it. The bad thing was that no matter what he said, Rachel would still be hurt.

He took the stairs two at a time and found Rachel in the nursery, rocking the baby. The picture of the two together always caused an ache in his chest.

"Rachel… I'm sorry. I should have wakened you this morning before I left."

Rachel didn't look at Cole as she continued to rock her daughter. She was too hurt by his attitude. She just remained silent as she got up and laid little Hannah in the bed. When she turned around, Cole was gone. She found him in the guest room, packing up his things.

"I'm moving back to the bunkhouse."

It was more than that. Cole was leaving her altogether.

Rachel had never felt hurt like this. "You're not sorry. You didn't want to face me, or face your own feelings."

He paused from gathering his things. "I wish it could be different, Rachel."

"Darn you, Cole. It can be different, but you have to want it. You have to want me bad enough to fight for me."

His eyes grew fierce. "You don't think I've tried? Every time I reach for something, it gets snatched away. You get a little tired of trying." He zipped the bag. "It's better this way."

Rachel followed him downstairs but wasn't about to beg him to stay. They reached the kitchen when the phone rang and she picked it up.

"Hello," she said.

"Hello, Rachel, it's Beth Nealey."

She wiped the tears from her eyes. "Beth, how are you?" She didn't want to talk now.

"I'm fine. And I hope you are, too, since I have some news for you." There was a sigh. "I've located Josh's father."

# CHAPTER TEN

AN HOUR later, Rachel couldn't sit still any longer and went out to the porch to wait for Beth's arrival. She'd hoped that Amy and Josh wouldn't return at least until Beth and she could figure out the situation. The last thing she wanted was the boy to get caught in the middle.

"It's going to be all right, Rachel," Cole said as he stepped out the door and stood at the railing.

"How can you say that?" She didn't want any kind words from him. He was leaving her, too. "What kind of man leaves his son without any food or money? And now, he wants to take Josh away from a secure home and family." She blinked at her welling tears. "He's part of the family."

"I know," Cole said. "The boy belongs here with you. And Beth will see that, too. I doubt she'll hand over Josh to the man who deserted him."

He reached for her and Rachel didn't resist as he pulled her against his chest. She needed his strength, his support, if just for a little while. Cy came across the yard to the porch as Beth Nealey's familiar sedan drove up to the house.

Rachel moved out of Cole's embrace and put on a smile as she walked down the steps to greet her. Beth got out of the car as a tall gaunt man climbed out of the passenger side. He looked years older than his probable age of early forties. No doubt Sam Owens had lived a hard life.

As far as Rachel was concerned that didn't matter. No parent should ever abandon his child. There were no circumstances that could excuse it.

"Beth, welcome," Rachel said.

The social worker took her hand. "It's good to see you, Rachel. How is little Hannah doing?"

"Growing like a weed. She's asleep right now."

"I'll look in on her later." She nodded to Cole who had followed Rachel down the steps, then greeted Cy.

The man in question walked toward them and Beth did the introductions. "Rachel Hewitt, this is Sam Owens."

Mr. Owens held his hat in his hands and nodded. "Hello, ma'am. I sure do appreciate you carin' for my boy all this time."

"Josh is a joy to have here." Rachel was angry, but refused to lose control.

Sam glanced around toward the corral. "Is the boy around?"

Rachel paused. "He's running some errands for me in town."

Sam nodded. "He's a hard worker."

Before Rachel could respond, Beth said, "Maybe we should go inside…and talk."

Cole opened the door and everyone walked into the kitchen. "Would anyone like coffee?" he asked, then started taking down the cups.

Once everyone sat at the table and the mugs were passed out, Rachel spoke first. "Mr. Owens, I need to know how you could leave your son alone."

The older man's blue eyes were so much like his son's. "There wasn't much I could do. I had to find work."

"Then why not take Josh with you?"

Sam's gaze darted to Beth, then back to Rachel. "You know, ma'am, this time of year ranch work is scarce. But then I heard about a job trailing a large herd on a spread by Midland. But I'd have to stay in a line shack in the middle of nowhere." He paused. "There was no room for Josh. But I swear I left him with food and what money I had left, and I was sending him money home from every paycheck."

"I don't believe that," Rachel said. "Josh was half starved when he came here."

He nodded. "And that's somethin' I'll regret as long as I live. But the person I trusted to send money back here to Josh didn't do it." He tossed a glance at Beth who motioned for him to continue the story. "The ranch foreman was to take most of my pay and mail it here to Josh." He lowered his head. "You see…I can't write very well, so he was helping me. Later, I found out that he was helping himself to more by pocketing my money. When I found out, I quit and came back and heard Miss Nealey was looking for me."

"I checked out his story," Beth said. "Seems this foreman had pulled this with other ranch hands, too. But I told Sam that doesn't excuse him from leaving his underage son alone. And he can't have custody until he can prove that he can provide a home for his son."

"I need to find work." Sam looked at the social worker. "But you said I could see Josh today."

"Yes, we can work out some kind of visitation with Rachel." Beth turned to her. "Do you have a problem with that?"

Rachel shook her head. "No, but I want Josh to go back to school."

Sam echoed. "I want that, too. He's a smart boy."

Just then Rachel heard the old truck pull up to the back door. "That's Josh."

Sam's eyes watered. "Please, can I go see my boy?"

Rachel nodded, and the older man nearly ran out the door.

Beth moved to Rachel's side. "I think Sam is basically a good man. He just needs a little help finding direction." She sighed as she glanced out the window to see father and son embrace. "Some days I love my job. I think I'll go upstairs and see Hannah."

"Sure," Rachel told her. "She should be waking up soon."

After the social worker left, Rachel couldn't keep from going to see Josh. She glanced across the room at Cole, but his expression gave no clue to what he was thinking.

"Are you okay?" he asked.

*No*! She ignored his question and walked to the back door and watched the scene between the father and son through the screen.

Josh was hugging his father and jabbering away. Then he introduced Amy to Sam. Rachel's throat tightened when she saw how Sam's smile took ages off the man.

There was no doubt about the love between the two. They needed to be together.

"Well, it looks like some things turn out happily," she murmured, mostly to herself, knowing that she was losing another person she loved.

Josh looked up as she walked out on the porch. "Hey, Rachel. My dad came back."

His teary smile made it difficult for her to talk. "I know, isn't it great." At least something had turned out right.

She looked over her shoulder to find Cole watching her. And some things don't. She'd given herself to the man last night. She'd offered him everything, but he didn't want her. No matter how much she loved him, she couldn't make him stay here.

It was time to let him go.

Before she lost her nerve, she turned back to father and son. "Hey, Sam."

The man looked at her. "Yes, ma'am."

"You say you're looking for work?"

"Yes, ma'am, I am. Do you know of anyone hiring?"

"I am. Seems I have a position here that just opened up."

Josh's eyes widened. Sam looked unconvinced.

"It comes with a room in the bunkhouse and meals included. What do you say?"

"Thank you, Miss Hewitt. I'm most grateful. You won't be sorry."

She already was. "Good. Please, call me Rachel. You can move in anytime."

Rachel turned around to see Cole leaning against the post on the porch. If he was surprised, he didn't show it. Of course, he was pretty good at hiding his feelings. "Looks like you got your wish, I've found your replacement. So now you can finally move on."

Twenty minutes later, Cole was tossing clothes into his duffel bag. He didn't need to be asked twice to leave. He grabbed his shaving kit, and worked it into the corner of the nylon bag and glanced around. There wasn't much else.

He was out of here.

"So you're really leaving."

Cole turned to the doorway to see Cy. "It's time."

"For a drifter, it's past time," the old man told him. "Of course, it seems you found ways to keep from moving on."

Cole didn't want to argue. "Rachel doesn't need me anymore."

"Rachel doesn't think she needs anyone. It's all for show, though—to protect her heart." He frowned. "Don't blame her. A lot of people have let her down. She's gotten so she doesn't expect anyone to stick around."

Cole zipped the bag. He knew the feeling all too well. "I'm not the man she needs."

The foreman stared at him. "So you're just going to leave her to Wills, or worse yet, that has-been jock, Vince."

Cole didn't want to think about Rachel with another man. Not after he'd had a taste of her loving. The way she kissed him, the way she gave herself to him… Just last night he'd held her in his arms as she cried out in passion. A shiver raced through him, and he pushed aside the thought.

"Rachel's got common sense. She'll do what's best for her and Hannah." He picked up his bag and headed for the door. "I've got to go."

That's when Josh rushed in. "Rachel said you're leaving." The boy glanced down at the bag in his hand.

"I've been planning to leave all along. Your dad coming back was just good timing. He can replace me."

"But I thought…you and Rachel. I mean I thought you wanted to stay because of her." The teenager looked panicked. "I know you care about her…and Hannah. And what about me…?"

Cole had no answers for Josh, or himself. If things could be different…if he was different. "This is something I have to do. I have a place back in Atlanta…a business. I've been gone a long time and I need to get back to it."

Josh didn't say anything.

"I want you to take care of Rachel, and stay in school."

The boy nodded, not hiding the tears in his eyes.

When Cole held out his hand to shake it, Josh ignored it and threw his arms around Cole. "Thanks for helping me out. I'll never forget you." He broke off the embrace and ran out.

Cole's heart seemed to lodge in his throat. He had to get out, now.

"Seems you've made an impression on the boy."

He shrugged. "I just talked to him a few times. But he'll do okay."

Cy held out his hand and Cole took it. "I owe you a lot, Parrish. My life. I wish things could be different."

"They can't," Cole told him, barely holding it together.

The older man studied him for a long time. "Maybe someday you'll realize that everything you were looking for was right here."

Cole could only nod, then he walked out the door. He glanced up at the house, but this time, Rachel wasn't on the porch. His gaze moved higher and he spotted her in the window, holding Hannah.

Something slammed into his chest. And yet, he kept walking toward the truck, telling himself this was for the best. Tossing his bag in the back, he jumped in, and started the engine, driving off.

What was most painful, Rachel was everything he could ever want...and love.

And he couldn't do a damn thing about it.

"This isn't working," Luke Calloway said as he walked into Cole's office at C & P Fiber Optics.

Cole had been back in Atlanta for nearly a month.

He moved back into his old condo, back to his position at the C&P Fiber Optics Company. He did it all but still couldn't forget his time in Texas.

"What isn't working?"

"You... You don't want to be here."

His longtime friend had the charm and good looks that got everyone's attention. He knew how to handle the customers and play the game, and Luke loved it all.

Cole liked working behind the scenes, making the operation run smoothly. "I know I'm a little rusty..."

Luke shook his head. "That's not the problem. You're like a robot—moving from here to there, but with no passion."

Cole swallowed. His partner was right, but there was nowhere else for him to go. "It's just taken me a while to adjust to being back."

Luke studied him. "I wish that were true. I can't tell you how badly I want my friend and partner here. But I can see how much you hate being cooped up all day." He paused. "Your heart isn't in the business. It's back in Texas... with Rachel."

Cole's chest tightened. "Don't go there."

"You never left. And don't deny you haven't been thinking about her."

Cole tried to act indignant over the crazy talk, but he could never fool Luke. They'd shared too much over the years. "Okay, so I think about Rachel. That doesn't mean I'm going to do anything about it. I mean, I couldn't saddle her with someone with my history. That's the reason I left in the first place."

"Funny thing, when it comes to love, it seems that women overlook a lot of our faults."

"No, I'm serious," Cole said. "I can't give her what she wants. A family man."

"You could if you'd just forgive yourself and put the past where it belongs." Luke pointed his finger at him. "Listen to me, Cole. No matter what accusations Jillian threw at you, you were both to blame for the failure of your marriage." Luke came around the desk and sat on the edge. "You gave her a lot, but she could never put up with sharing you with anything, or anybody else. That included me."

Cole knew Jillian was possessive, and found ways to keep him from his friends. "But if I'd been there for her…"

"It wouldn't have changed anything. It was a terrible thing that happened to your baby, but you have to forgive yourself, and let it go. Move on."

"What if I can't?"

Luke grew serious. "How bad do you want a life with this woman?"

"More than anything I've ever wanted."

"Then go for it. As much as I'd love to keep you here with me, you belong with Rachel. She's gotten under your skin—in a good way." A smile creased Luke's mouth. "I bet she's good-looking, too. I remember talking with her on the phone. That lazy, smoky voice of hers had me fantasizing about all sorts of things…"

Cole hated Luke's lecherous look. "Stop it. She's not like that, and she's definitely not used to guys like you." His friend had a notorious reputation with women.

"Well, aren't you being defensive." Luke raised an eyebrow. "I think, pal, that's called love. So are you going to wise up and go after her, or sit around here and make my life miserable?"

As much as Cole tried not to, he'd fallen in love with Rachel…and Hannah. He ached so much for them. He couldn't help but wonder what she'd done to the ranch. Had she started with her plans? And Duke. He'd missed him and their rides together… with Rachel beside him.

He glanced at Luke. "You still have someone interested in buying me out?"

His friend gave a slow nod. "Or we can keep things here as they are for a while longer. I can run things."

Cole knew that was making it too easy for him. "No, Luke, I'm finished drifting." He released a sigh. "I'm finally ready to go home. That is, if Rachel will have me."

# CHAPTER ELEVEN

HOT August turned into an even hotter September, and the weather didn't agree with Rachel at all. She hadn't wanted to analyze the reason for her lack of appetite and sleeplessness, but in her heart she couldn't deny it was Cole.

She climbed out of bed. She needed to get the day started, no matter how she felt. People depended on her. She had Hannah to feed, breakfast to make for Cy, Josh and Sam.

For everyone but…Cole.

She chided herself for her melancholy mood as she slipped on her robe. After checking on a still-sleeping Hannah she took a quick shower and got dressed for the day.

In the kitchen she set Hannah's carrier on the table and began to prepare her daughter's food. Since her last checkup, it was rice cereal mixed with formula.

Lately there were very few things that made Rachel smile. Hannah was at the top of her list. She unlocked and opened the back door, already feeling the early-morning heat. She waved at Cy and Sam who were headed toward the barn to start the chores.

She went back to the table and began to spoon-feed Hannah. Rachel had to grin at the child's antics. Her hands and feet were motoring at high speed. In between bites she cooed at her mother.

"Well, you sure are happy this morning. Yes, you are," Rachel cooed right back.

Meal completed, she washed off the baby, then lifted her daughter out of the carrier to feed her a bottle. That was when she heard a vehicle pull up outside. Who would come visiting so early?

Carrying Hannah, Rachel went to the doorway. She squinted into the bright sunlight and saw a familiar black truck hauling a horse trailer. Cole's truck. Her breath caught and her pulse pounded loudly in her ears as she watched him climb out of the cab. Josh came running out of the bunkhouse to greet him.

Rachel froze as he climbed the steps to the porch. He was dressed in dark jeans with a pale blue, starched Western-style shirt. He wore that familiar black hat that covered his thick nearly black hair. And when he removed it, she noticed he'd gotten a haircut.

She searched his face…she was hungry for any glimpse of the man. For those smoky-gray eyes that hid so much, his sexy cleft chin, and his tempting mouth. Suddenly she recalled the pain he'd caused when he'd walked away from her.

"Look, Rachel," Josh began as he hurried up behind Cole. "Cole's back."

"I can see that," she managed.

"Here, let me take Hannah," the teenager said as he scooped the baby from her arms and disappeared into the house, leaving Rachel defenseless. She had no place to go…to escape.

Cole knew he should have called first but he was afraid Rachel would hang up on him, and he wouldn't blame her. He'd put her through a lot.

"Hello, Rachel."

"Cole." She nodded. "If you're looking for work, I'm sorry. I'm not hiring right now."

"I'm not here for a job." His gaze searched her beautiful face. Those big brown eyes that had haunted him every hour of every day since he'd left her. "I came to talk with you."

Her eyes widened. "What in the world would you want to talk with me about? You made your feelings perfectly clear…you wanted to leave."

She wasn't going to make this easy for him. "What if I told you I realize that I was wrong?" he asked. "What if I realized that everything I want is right here?"

She shook her head. There were tears in her eyes. "Don't do this, Cole. Just do us both a favor and turn around and leave."

She started to return to the kitchen when he touched her arm. "Rachel, please, I know I don't deserve your attention, but I need it. I didn't come back to hurt you."

"No, you did that when you left."

He wasn't sure he could give her the answer she wanted. "Because there were so many things in my past that I'd left unresolved. I ran away because I hadn't faced them. I blamed myself for everything that happened in my marriage. I'd lost so much that I was afraid to risk again. I was afraid to trust my feelings."

Rachel stood strong. "What does that have to do with me?"

He swallowed. "I want a chance with you. I know I don't deserve it but, please, Rachel, don't turn me away."

"How can I believe you when a month ago you walked away? I can't do this again, Cole." She turned, but hesitated when Hannah cried. Instead she headed off to the far side of the porch and sank down on the old swing.

Cole had followed her and sat on the railing across from her. "I needed that time, Rachel. I needed time to heal from my past. So I went back to Atlanta and I tried to work at my company."

Her head shot up. "Your company?"

He nodded. He'd never told her anything about himself. "About ten years ago my friend, Luke, and I started a company, C & P Fiber Optics."

"All this time I thought you were a ranch hand." She shook her head. "Did I ever know you, Cole?"

He leaned closer. "Oh, Rachel, you knew me better than anyone. Better than I knew myself."

She drew a shaky breath as she rose and gripped the corner post. "I bet Luke is happy to have you back."

"He was at first, but lately, he's been more than ready to shove me out the door."

"Why? It's your company, too."

He nodded. "At one time the company was my life, but it's not what I want anymore. That's the reason I decided to sell my half to Luke."

He hesitated, but he had to tell Rachel everything. "I also went to see Jillian. We talked through a lot of things…a lot of pain. I apologized for not being there for her." He drew a long breath and released it. "She apologized, too. She said she had no right to blame me for the loss of our baby."

Rachel could still see the strain on his face. She fought to keep from going to him. "Do you believe her?"

He nodded. "In my head I do, but there will always be a place in my heart…that will still hold the pain."

She blinked back tears. "Of course, he was your son."

He nodded, but she could see the raw emotions.

"Do you still love her?"

Cole looked surprised at her question. "No." He smiled softly. "In fact she's remarried…and expecting a child." He didn't hesitate to continue to say, "And I'm happy she's moved on with her life." His eyes held hers. "Now, I want to move on with mine."

Rachel swallowed the sudden dryness in her throat. "What are you going to do now?"

"I'm done drifting, that's for sure. I plan to go into the horse breeding business."

She tried to hide her disappointment with attitude. "What does that have to do with you showing up here?"

"Well, now that you have the financial means I know you have a lot of plans for the Bar H. I want to add to those." He paused. "I thought we could be partners. Besides raising cattle, we could breed quarter horses…together. Duke would sire some incredible foals."

He wanted her—but only as a business partner. "I'm sorry, Cole, I don't think it is a good idea."

"If you're worried about capital…I assure you that I can invest—"

"You don't get it," she interrupted. He couldn't be that dense, she thought. "We made love. Maybe it didn't mean anything to you, but it did to me. I can't just brush that aside as if it never happened and go into business with you now."

She started to move by him, when Cole reached for her. "It meant everything to me, Rachel." Although she tried to get by him, he managed to keep her from leaving. "You are everything to me. I don't just want to go into business with you, I want to build a future with you…with Hannah. I just wanted to prove to you that I was going to put down roots here…for good." He cupped her face, and his eyes were as tender as his words. "Oh, Rachel, I was a fool to leave you. But I couldn't give you what you needed before now."

Her resolve was fading fast. "I only need you, Cole. Only you."

"I love you," he breathed. He captured her mouth in a scorching kiss. He pulled her close letting her feel the heat between them. She whimpered, floating on sensations he was stirring within her. He tasted her, showing how much he desired her.

Finally he broke away. "Tell me I'm not too late…"

She smiled in between eager kisses. "That all depends. Tell me what kind of partnership you're looking for."

He smiled, too. "Definitely a long-term commitment."

Her arms slipped around his neck. "I think this deal might take some serious negotiations."

"I was hoping you'd say that," he said and kissed her again and again.

Rachel's head was spinning. "Say it again."

He raised his head, revealing those silver-gray eyes. "I love you, Rachel."

She felt tears sting her eyes. "I love you, too, Cole. I thought you were never coming back…"

"I'm sorry…" He kissed the tears from her cheeks. "I couldn't come to you until I'd dealt with my past. It was you that helped me do that."

"I'm glad," she whispered against his mouth. Then she gave into the kiss as he lifted her in his arms, making her feel his want and need for her.

A whinnying sound finally broke them apart. "Oh, I forgot about Sassy. You've got to see her, Rachel. She's a beautiful mare I found to breed with Duke. But she lives up to her name, as you can see, and she's been cooped up in the trailer for hours."

This time the horse kicked at the side. "She doesn't sound happy. We better go get her."

They walked along the porch and started for the steps when Josh came out the back door, carrying a crying baby. "I can't get Hannah to stop." He looked panicked as he started to hand the restless bundle to Rachel.

"Let me have her," Cole said as he took the squirming baby from the teenager. "Josh, will you go take the mare from the trailer, and put her in a stall in the barn?"

The boy glanced at Rachel, then back at Cole. "You staying?"

"If Rachel will have me."

Never taking her eyes off Cole, Rachel said, "Josh, you better get the mare into the barn."

"All right!" the teenager yelled. He jumped off the steps and ran toward the trailer.

Cole placed Hannah against his shoulder and patted her back. She calmed immediately. He grinned. "I guess I still got it."

A thrill shot through Rachel as she watched the man who moments ago kissed her senseless, and now, was cuddling a baby in his arms.

"I meant what I said, Rachel. I love you…and Hannah. I want to marry you and for us to be a family."

"Are you sure, Cole?"

He gave a firm nod. "You are all I ever thought about since I left here. I would never have come back if I wasn't sure."

Cole knew he was a lucky guy, he also knew he had a lot to make up to Rachel. He smiled and dug into his pocket. "I had big plans to wine and dine you later in town, but I can't wait." He pulled out a solitaire diamond ring.

"Oh, Cole, it's beautiful."

"Nothing can compare to you. Will you marry me, Rachel?"

Her eyes met his. "Oh, yes, Cole, I'll marry you."

He managed to slip the ring on, then leaned down and kissed her tenderly. He pulled away, searching her face. "Maybe we should put Hannah down for a nap. Then we can work on those negotiations you suggested…"

"I'd like that…very much." She looped her hand through his arm and together they headed for the door.

Cole looked out as Josh opened the trailer. He caught Cy coming from the barn to help. He looked toward the house and waved. "Welcome home, Cole," the older man called.

"Thanks, Cy. It's good to be back." He looked down at Rachel and pulled her against him. Yes, it was good to be home… For good.

## EPILOGUE

"YOU think you're hot stuff, don't you, old guy?"

Cole watched Duke prance around the corral. The stallion whinnied his impatience for the in-season mare housed in the new breeding barn.

In the past twelve months, the horse had made quite a reputation for the Bar H Ranch's new breeding program. Duke's first sire had been from Sassy, who produced a pretty little filly Rachel had aptly named Drifter's Lady.

Cole couldn't help but look around at all the changes that had taken place in the past year since his return.

It was summertime. Eighteen months since he'd first shown up at the broken-down cattle ranch, asking Rachel Hewitt for a job.

Now with all the repairs finished, there was a freshly painted barn and a new corral along with whitewashed outbuildings and recently constructed breeding stables. And he and Rachel had more plans for the ranch. Nothing was going to stop the progress to rebuild the Bar H. To turn it into a showplace once again.

He glanced over his shoulder to the shiny painted white house with deep burgundy shutters. The rebuilt porch was adorned with baskets of flowers held along the eaves. A new swing had been added where he and his bride sat most evenings.

They'd married practically right away in Rachel's small church, then had the reception right here at the ranch. He hadn't wanted to give Rachel a chance to decide he wasn't worth it, and change her mind.

Luke had made the trip and stood in as his best man. And surprisingly, his friend had made two other trips back to the ranch. Of course, the Campbells's oldest daughter, Megan, returning home to teach school might have had a lot to do with those visits. Who knows? Maybe his workaholic friend might even slow down and enjoy life, too.

Cole saw the back door open and Rachel came outside into the sunlight with little Hannah in tow. His pulse raced as usual whenever he saw his family. His wife and daughter. Just a few months ago, they'd legally adopted Hannah. It was hard to believe that she was a year old and toddling around. He loved to hear her say dada.

Amy walked out of the barn and took charge of the baby. After they exchanged a conversation, Rachel headed toward him. He felt his body stir as his beautiful wife smiled. He jumped down from the corral railing and met her halfway. He drew her into his arms and kissed her long and hard. "Good morning," he breathed against her mouth.

Rachel pulled back, her eyes sparkling. "You

already wished me good morning…before you got out of bed."

He groaned, recalling their predawn lovemaking. "Would I be greedy to say I want to take you back there right now?"

"Only if you repeat this morning." She raised an eyebrow. "But I think we're going to have to find another place to go to be alone. The house is near full right now. Amy is playing with Hannah, and you know wherever Amy is Josh is close by."

There were also a few more ranch hands hired to help around the Bar H, including Sam Owens. As it turned out Josh's father was good with horses. Best of all, Cy's workload was lighter.

"Isn't he going off to college soon?"

She looked sad. "Don't remind me. Both Amy and Josh will be gone before we know it."

Josh had surprised them and aced his senior year in high school. He'd gotten a partial scholarship to college in Houston. "You gave him a future, Rachel, when you took him in."

"You helped, too. I love you for giving him the money for school."

Money would never be a problem for either of them. "It's the only way to be alone with you." Cole pulled Rachel into a tight embrace. "I think I'm going to talk to the contractor to see if he can build us a secret hideaway."

She smiled up at him. "That could be fun." She grew serious. "Because soon things are going to get a little more crowded around here."

"Why's that?"

"Seems that the mares aren't the only ones who'll be delivering a baby in the winter."

Rachel held her breath while she watched her news sink in. They'd planned to wait until the ranch was finished, but there had been a few times… "I just took a pregnancy test. It came out positive. I guess we weren't so careful." Why didn't he say anything? "Cole, please, I know we didn't plan this."

His mouth covered hers and broke off anything she was about to say. When he released her, they were both breathless.

"How did I get so lucky?" He kissed her again. "I love you, Rachel. And I already love our baby."

"We're both lucky," she said. "The day you showed up here everything changed for me."

"It did for me, too. I'd been drifting for so long and I knew the minute I saw you, I should move on. But as you know, I couldn't go."

Rachel knew that Cole had concerns about her pregnancy. "It's going to be okay this time, Cole."

He nodded. "I know. And I'm going to be there for you every step of the way." He kissed her. "It took me a while, but you showed me nothing is more important than family." He grinned. "The bigger the better."

\* \* \* \* \*

*Love Inspired*
# HISTORICAL

*Powerful, engaging stories of romance,
adventure and faith
set in the past—when life was simpler
and faith played
a major role in everyday lives.*

*Turn the page for a sneak preview of
THE BRITON
by
Catherine Palmer*

*Love Inspired Historical—love and faith
throughout the ages
A brand-new line from Steeple Hill Books
Launching this February!*

"Welcome to the family, Briton," said one of Olaf's men in a mocking voice. "We look forward to the presence of a woman at our hall."

Bronwen grasped her tunic and yanked it from the Viking's thick fingers. As she stepped away from the table, she heard the drunken laughter of the barbarians behind her. How could her father have betrothed her to the old Viking?

Running down the stone steps toward the heavy oak door that led outside from the keep, Bronwen gathered her mantle about her. She ordered the doorman to open the door, and he did so reluctantly, pressing her to carry a torch. But Bronwen pushed past him and fled into the darkness.

Dashing down the steep, pebbled hill toward the beach, she felt the frozen ground give way to sand. She threw off her veil and circlet and kicked away her shoes.

Racing alongside the pounding surf, she felt hot tears of anger and shame well up and stream down her cheeks. With no concern for her safety, Bronwen ran and ran—her long braids streaming behind her, falling loose, drifting like a tattered black flag.

Blinded with weeping, she did not see the dark form that sprang up in her path and stopped dead her headlong sprint. Bronwen shrieked in surprise and fear as iron arms pinned her, and a heavy cloak threatened to suffocate her.

"Release me!" she cried. "Guard! Guard, help me."

"Hush, my lady." A deep voice emanated from the darkness. "I mean you no harm. What demon drives you to run through the night without fear for your safety?"

"Release me, villain! I am the daughter—"

"I shall hold you until you calm yourself. We had heard there were witches in Amounderness, but I had not thought to meet one so openly."

Still held tight in the man's arms, Bronwen drew back and peered up at the hooded figure. "You! You are the man who spied on our feast. Release me at once, or I shall call the guard upon you."

The man chuckled at this and turned toward his companions, who stood in a group nearby. Bronwen caught hold of the back of his hood and jerked it down to reveal a head of glossy raven curls. But the man's face was shrouded in darkness yet, and as he looked at her, she could not read his expression.

"So you are the blessed bride-to-be." He returned the hood to his head. "Your father has paired you with an interesting choice."

Relieved that her captor did not appear to be a

highwayman, she pushed away from him and sagged onto the wet sand. "Please leave me here alone. I need peace to think. Go on your way."

The tall stranger shrugged off his outer mantle and wrapped it around her shoulders. "Why did your father betroth you thus to the aged Viking?" he asked.

"For one purported to be a spy, you know precious little about Amounderness. But I shall tell you, as it is all common knowledge."

She pulled the cloak tightly about her, reveling in its warmth. "This land, known as Amounderness, once was Briton territory. Olaf Lothbrok, my betrothed, came here as a youth when the Viking invasions had nearly subsided. He took the lands directly to the south of Rossall Hall from their Briton lord. Then, of course, the Normans came, and Amounderness was pillaged by William the Conqueror's army."

The man squatted on the sand beside Bronwen. He listened with obvious interest as she continued. "When William took an account of Amounderness in his Domesday Book, he recorded no remaining lords and few people at all. But he did not know the Britons. Slowly we crept out of hiding and returned to our halls. My father's family reoccupied Rossall Hall. And there we live, as we should, watching over our serfs as they fish and grow their meager crops. Indeed, there is not much here for the greedy Normans to want, if they are the ones for whom you spy."

Unwilling to continue speaking when her heart was so heavy, Bronwen stood and turned toward the sea. The traveler rose beside her and touched her arm. "Olaf Lothbrok's lands—together with your father's—will reunite most of Amounderness under the rule of the son you are beholden to bear. A clever plan. Your sister's future husband holds the rest of the adjoining lands, I understand."

"You've done your work, sir. Your lord will be pleased. Who is he—some land-hungry Scottish baron? Or have you forgotten that King Stephen gave Amounderness to the Scots, as a trade for their support in his war with Matilda? I certainly hope your lord is not a Norman. He would be so disappointed to learn he has no legal rights here. Now, if you will excuse me?"

Bronwen turned and began walking back along the beach toward Rossall Hall. She felt better for her run, and somehow her father's plan did not seem so far-fetched anymore. Distant lights twinkled through the fog that was rolling in from the west, and she suddenly realized what a long way she had come.

"My lady," the man's voice called out behind her.

Bronwen kept walking, unwilling to face again the one who had seen her in her humiliation. She didn't care what he reported to his master.

"My lady, you have quite a walk ahead of you." The traveler strode forward to join her. "I shall accompany you to your destination."

"You leave me no choice, I see."

"I am not one to compromise myself, dear lady. I follow the path God has set before me and none other."

"And just who are you?"

"I am called Jacques."

"French. A Norman, as I had suspected."

The man chuckled. "Not nearly as Norman as you are Briton."

As they approached the fortress, Bronwen could see that the guests had not yet begun to disperse. Perhaps no one had missed her, and she could slip quietly into bed beside Gildan.

She turned to go, but he took her arm and studied her face in the moonlight. Then, gently, he drew her into the folds of his hooded cloak. "Perhaps the bride would like the memory of a younger man's embrace to warm her," he whispered.

Astonished, Bronwen attempted to remove his arms from around her waist. But she could not escape his lips as they found her own. The kiss was soft and warm, melting away her resistance like the sun upon the snow. Before she had time to react, he was striding back down the beach.

Bronwen stood stunned for a moment, clutching his woolen mantle about her. Suddenly she cried out, "Wait, Jacques! Your mantle!"

The dark one turned to her. "Keep it for now," he shouted into the wind. "I shall ask for it when we meet again."

\* \* \* \* \*

*Don't miss this deeply moving story,*
***THE BRITON,***
*available February 2008*
*from the new Love Inspired Historical line.*

*And also look for*
***HOMESPUN BRIDE***
*by Jillian Hart,*
*where a Montana woman discovers that love*
*is the greatest blessing of all.*

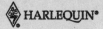
**HARLEQUIN®**

# EVERLASTING LOVE™

*Every great love has a story to tell™*

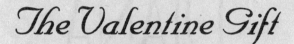

*The Valentine Gift*

**featuring
three deeply emotional
stories of love that stands
the test of time, just in time
for Valentine's Day!**

*USA TODAY* bestselling author
## Tara Taylor Quinn

## Linda Cardillo
and
## Jean Brashear

**Available just in time for Valentine's Day
February wherever you buy books.**

**www.eHarlequin.com**   HEL65427

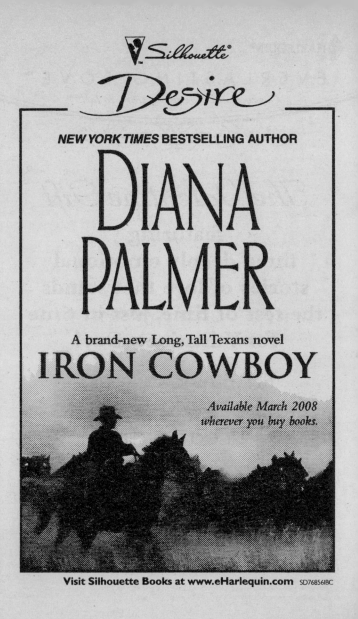

Silhouette®

*Desire*

**NEW YORK TIMES BESTSELLING AUTHOR**

# DIANA PALMER

A brand-new Long, Tall Texans novel

# IRON COWBOY

*Available March 2008
wherever you buy books.*

**Visit Silhouette Books at www.eHarlequin.com** SD76856IBC

**$1.**<sup>**00**</sup> **OFF**

The bestselling Lakeshore Chronicles continue with *Snowfall at Willow Lake*, a story of what comes after a woman survives an unspeakable horror and finds her way home, to healing and redemption and a new chance at happiness.

# SUSAN WIGGS

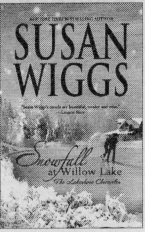

*On sale February 2008!*

---

**SAVE $1.**<sup>**00**</sup> off the purchase price of
**SNOWFALL AT WILLOW LAKE**
by Susan Wiggs.

Offer valid from February 1, 2008, to April 30, 2008.
Redeemable at participating retail outlets. Limit one coupon per purchase.

52608168

5 65373 00076 2 (8100) 0 11463

® and TM are trademarks owned and used by the trademark owner and/or its licensee.
© 2008 Harlequin Enterprises Limited

MSW2493CPN

# REQUEST YOUR FREE BOOKS!
## 2 FREE NOVELS PLUS 2
## FREE GIFTS!

### From the Heart, For the Heart

HR07

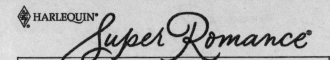

# Texas Hold 'Em

### When it comes to love, the stakes are high

Sixteen years ago, Luke Chisum dated
Becky Parker on a dare...before going
on to break her heart. Now the former
River Bluff daredevil is back, rekindling
desire and tempting Becky to pick up
where they left off. But this time she has
to resist or Luke could discover the secret
she's kept locked away all these years....

*Look for*

# TEXAS BLUFF

### *by Linda Warren*

#### #1470

*Available February 2008
wherever you buy books.*

# HARLEQUIN *Romance*

## Coming Next Month

**Ranchers, lords, sheikhs and playboys—the perfect men to make you sigh this Valentine's Day, from Harlequin Romance®...**

### #4003 CATTLE RANCHER, SECRET SON  Margaret Way

Have you ever fallen in love at first sight? Gina did—but she knew she could never be good enough for Cal's society family. Now Cal's determined to marry her—but is it to avoid a scandal and claim his son, or because he really loves her?

### #4004 RESCUED BY THE SHEIKH  Barbara McMahon
*Desert Brides*

Be swept away to the swirling sands and cool oases of the Moquansaid desert. Lost and alone, Lisa is relieved to be rescued by a handsome stranger. But this sheikh is no ordinary man, and Lisa suddenly begins to feel out of her depth again....

### #4005 THE PLAYBOY'S PLAIN JANE  Cara Colter

You know the type: confident, sexy, gorgeous—and he knows it. Entrepreneur Dylan simply has *it*. But Katie's no pushover and is determined to steer clear—that is until she starts to see a side of him she never knew existed.

### #4006 HER ONE AND ONLY VALENTINE  Trish Wylie

Do you find yourself hoping for a special surprise on Valentine's Day? Single mom Rhiannon's about to get a big one! When Kane left, breaking Rhiannon's heart, he didn't know he'd left behind something infinitely precious. But now he's back in town....

### #4007 ENGLISH LORD, ORDINARY LADY  Fiona Harper
*By Royal Appointment*

It's so important to be loved for who you *really* are inside. Josie agrees, and thinks new boss Will doesn't look beneath the surface enough. But appearances can be deceptive, especially when moonlit kisses in the castle orchard get in the way!

### #4008 EXECUTIVE MOTHER-TO-BE  Nicola Marsh
*Baby on Board*

Career-girl Kristen's spontaneous decision to share one special night with sexy entrepreneur Nathan was crazy—and totally out of character! But now there are two shocks in store—one unexpected baby and one sexy but very familiar new boss....

HRCNM0108